Karl Olsberg

Cubeworld

A Minecraft Novel

TJ PUHL

Dedicated to Notch

Thanks to Nikolaus, who told me about Minecraft,
to Konstantin, who showed me how it works,
and to Leopold, the great architect,
who pointed out lots of mistakes in this story
and helped me correct them.

1.

Something's wrong, but I don't know what.

I don't even know how I know that there's something wrong. It's just a strange feeling that the world isn't quite like it should be.

The world is a beach, with some terrace-like hills behind it. Waves wash silently against the sand. A cool breeze comes in from the sea. The air smells of salt.

The trees – birches, with gray and white stems dotted with black patches – irritate me somehow.

I look down and get a jolt.

Where my hands should be, my arms end in square stumps.

Square. That's what's bothering me: The world is made of cubes. There are no curves, no soft transitions. The slopes of the hills don't rise gradually, but in precisely aligned steps. Even the leaves on the trees are arranged in neat cubic blocks.

Blocks. The word tickles my memory, but when I search it, I find nothing but emptiness. There are words and concepts in my head, but no memories. I don't know where I am and how I got here. I don't even remember my name.

But I'm not afraid. That's another strange fact. It's obvious to me that this world is not the one I'm supposed to be in, but I still feel comfortable. It's okay to be here.

I look up. Rectangular clouds move across a blue sky. A square sun sits low above the horizon. Although I look directly at it, my eyes don't hurt.

Do I have eyes at all? I'm not sure. I can't blink, but at least I can see.

I take a step. The sand feels warm, but as I look back,

there is no footprint behind me.

No wonder, since I don't even have feet. My legs are straight, rectangular sticks that I can bend back and forth only at my hips. Like my arms, they end in square stumps.

A picture flashes from the foggy depths of my memory, transparent and elusive like mist. I'm at a costume party. I wear a knight's armor. The visor of my helmet limits my sight. My arms and legs are encased in plastic. I stumble over something on the floor, maybe a bottle of beer, and crash down. Somebody's laughing.

That was in a different world, where everything was soft and imperfect. At the time, the stiff armor felt strange. But now my rectangular limbs feel natural, as if I have never had anything else.

What happened? The question is rapping at the back of my brain like a headache. There's something else that's bothering me, a vague feeling of danger. Something is very wrong, but the more I think about it, the less I can take hold of it.

All right, standing here brooding won't help. At least there appears to be no immediate danger.

I walk a few steps along the beach, then jump up one of the steps and onto a green surface. Grass? No, it's more like the ground is covered with rubber that's been painted with patches of different greens.

Jumping is easy. Am I weightless? I try bouncing up and down a few times. Every time I'm pulled back to the ground. I can't float.

It's walking, then.

I wander between cubic trees, when I see sudden movement ahead of me. Something scurries through the shade of the trees.

I walk toward it and discover some kind of white box with four columns as legs. At one end, there's a small cube, painted with rectangular spots in brown, pink, white, and black. The eyes (if those black and white spots are indeed eyes) seem to point in two different directions. It looks quite ridiculous, but I'm not feeling like laughing.

I probably wouldn't have guessed what it is if not for a definitely sheeplike sound that the thing – I'm not sure whether I should really call it an animal – makes: a rasping *baaah*. The cube head briefly turns in my direction, then the white box wanders off, not without baaing a few times in an annoyed manner.

At least there are other inhabitants in this world, even though they appear a bit unfinished. Then again, that term may very well apply to me – I can only guess that my own face doesn't look much brighter than that of the box sheep.

While I climb up the stairs of the hill, I sum up the possible explanations for my situation:

1. A dream. It's a possibility that can never really be ruled out; there are people who say that life is nothing but a dream and when we die we awake in reality. (While I think about it, I ask myself where I heard about that idea – I can't remember any people actually talking about it.) Pinching myself doesn't solve the problem, because it is entirely possible to dream about pinching yourself. But still, the world around me feels much too real. If this is a dream, it's a very uncommon one.

2. Drugs. I know there are drugs, but I don't know what they can do to you – as far as I know, I never took any. Beyond that, see dream hypothesis.

3. A hidden camera. Sometime, maybe in a former life, that concept had meaning. People were in situations that

appeared quite surreal to them, like my own situation seems to me right now. Then came the explanation: It was just some practical joke performed by the hidden camera team. Most of the time, this was really funny, at least for all but the subject of the joke. I don't remember much more about it, but I can't imagine how someone would be able to perform a trick like this on me.

4. A ... how was it called? A word beginning with *s*. Something to do with illusion, and with ... machines ... Strange. As soon as I try to get hold of words, they seem to hurry away into the most remote corners of my mind like frightened rabbits. It's as if something inside me tries to prevent me from thinking clearly. I try to feel around my face, looking for something that sits in front of my eyes, blocking my view of the real world. But without hands, I can't get a grip on anything.

5. Speaking of strange: Maybe everything I see is quite real and something weird happened to the world. Possibly a failed experiment at CERN's Large Hadron Collider particle accelerator, some physical phenomenon that has suspended the known laws of nature and turned everything into cubes. Okay, I don't know much about physics, but that sounds a little farfetched, doesn't it? On the other hand, I heard that scientists have no idea what 70 percent of the universe is made of. Cubes, maybe?

This doesn't lead anywhere. I can neither prove nor disprove any of these possibilities. Most likely, they're altogether wrong. Whatever the solution to this riddle may be, if there is one at all, I should start concentrating on the issues at hand, cubic or not.

In the meantime, the sun has climbed far up into the sky. That seems quick. It somehow makes me feel uneasy.

I reach the top of the hill and look around. To the left stretches a sandy desert, complete with cubic cacti. Behind it, an absurdly steep mountain range rises up. On the right, the forest continues for a while, until the trees open into a grassy plain with a lot of boxlike animals: black-and-white-patched beings easily identifiable as cows, and pink things that can only be pigs.

I decide to cross the desert in the direction of the mountains. Maybe from up there I can look even farther. I don't really know what I'm looking for. An exit, maybe? But an exit from what? And where could it lead?

Again, those useless thoughts spin around in my head so fast I feel sick. I push them away and concentrate on putting one foot in front of the other – metaphorically speaking, of course, since I don't have feet.

At the edge of the desert I come across another being. This one is much smaller than the sheep. Its cubic body rests on two narrow legs. On its head is a rectangular kind of duck's beak, with a red tongue dangling from it. The sound it makes, however, resembles the cackle of a chicken.

As I come nearer, the thing hops away, but it drops something: an egg.

This is the first nonrectangular object I discover in this world. Somehow, this raises my hopes. However, as if roundness were not compatible with the basic principles of this world, the egg isn't lying on the sandy ground. Instead, it floats slightly above it.

I take a step forward in order to examine this phenomenon, when something strange happens: There's a plop and the egg disappears like a bursting soap bubble. Confused, I look around, but all I can see is the chicken. It looks at me reproachfully, as if it disapproves of me being so careless toward its offspring.

But the egg hasn't disappeared completely. I can still feel it somewhere around.

Within me, to be specific.

Not in the sense that I have gulped it down or something. It's more like – a thought. I can't close my eyes, but when I concentrate on my inner vision, I can see it very clearly. And I can see something else: a boxy guy with a cyan-colored upper body, dark blue legs, and a squinting face that doesn't look any brighter than that of the sheep. It isn't me, is it?

A little scared, I look down at myself. My legs have the same dark blue color. I can't see what my torso looks like, but my handless arm-sticks confirm that I have just glimpsed a vision of myself.

What does that mean? And why do I have the feeling that the egg is somehow more than just a thought?

Immediately, I feel revulsion. I want to get rid of that thing. It works: The egg shoots out of my head as if my mind spat it out. It lands on top of a square of sand next to me, where it floats.

Cool trick!

I walk toward the egg, and again it disappears, only to manifest itself as a quite persistent thought in my mind. I spit it out again.

I wonder if this works with the duck-beaked chicken as well. It seems quite trusting, as if it knows that it has nothing to be afraid of – that it won't disappear. And indeed, it doesn't vanish when I get near it.

I look around. Maybe I can turn even more things into thoughts? How about sand, for example?

I'm trying to grab some sand, but I don't have hands. Frustrated, I beat on a block of sand in front of me. There is a crunching sound, and some cracks appear in its surface. After a moment, they disappear again.

Strange! I beat a couple of times on the block, until it vanishes with a soft plop. Instead, I now have a clear, sandy thought within me.

I turn around 90 degrees and think that it would be nice to place the sand block right there before me. But the block doesn't just appear. Instead, a smaller version of it materializes at the point where my right hand should be. Now I only need a second thought to turn the small cube into a large one on the ground.

I can't just walk through this world, I can change it!

But I realize that the light has shifted. While I played in the sandbox, the sun has moved far down toward the horizon. The blocks around me are cast in a yellowish light that quickly turns a bright orange.

The sunset takes less than a minute. Stars appear above me, and a pale, square moon rises. The world turns bluish gray.

Suddenly, I feel uncomfortable. I'm too old (I think) to be afraid of the dark, but still there is this nagging feeling that it's not good to run around here at night.

As if to prove my foreboding, I hear a groan that sounds like "*unngh.*" I turn and see a human figure approaching, its arms raised as if to welcome me. It resembles me in a way - the same boxlike arms and legs, the same dark blue trousers and light blue shirt - but the face doesn't look dumb; it looks positively evil, and the color of its flesh is a dark olive-green color.

"Hi!" I say. "Who are you?"

"*Unngh!*" the stranger answers.

He reaches me. As his outstretched arm touches me, I feel something like an electrical shock. It doesn't really hurt, but it sure feels uncomfortable.

I try to get away from this sinister fiend as quickly as I can, but now other beings come at me from all directions. Some look like twins of the guy with the green flesh, others like abstractions of human skeletons, armed with bows and arrows, which they fire at me.

The most friendly-looking being resembles a large rectangular cucumber that walks on four cubic little legs. As I run toward it, it greets me with a soft hiss. Frightened, I stop in my tracks. An arrow hits me and sends another electrical shock through my body.

The cucumber-man has almost reached me when his body seems to inflate like a balloon. A tremendous explosion shakes the world, and my body is shredded to pieces.

2.

Something's wrong, but I don't know what.

I don't even know how I know that there's something wrong. It's just a strange feeling that the world isn't quite like it should be.

The world is a beach, with some terrace-like hills behind it. Waves wash silently against the sand. A cool breeze comes in from the sea. The air smells of salt.

The fact that everything around me is made of cubes feels strange, although I don't really know why. Nothing is as it should be, but it still feels familiar. It's okay to be here.

I wander below cube trees, climb stairs up a hill, encounter a box sheep, and finally reach the top of the hill. To the left there are a desert and steep mountains. To the right, the forest thins into a plain dotted with black-and-white and pink toy animals.

Although I don't really know what I'm looking for, I decide to cross the desert to the mountains. From their peaks, I should have an even better view.

I come across a duck-beaked chicken, which drops an egg. Finally, something that's not rectangular! I discover that I can make the egg vanish into my mind and then make it appear again. Marvelous!

The sun sinks. Suddenly I get a strong sense of déjà vu: I've been here before. It's not good to be here, at least at night.

I collect a couple of sand blocks, saving them in my mind. I try to build a house with them, but that doesn't work, because I can't make a roof of sand. That's too bad, because now I hear a dull "*unngh*" somewhere near. A being that resembles me but appears less friendly approaches me with outstretched arms. Behind it there's a thing that looks like an upright cucumber walking on stumps. Skeletons come from the other direction.

Not good. Not good at all.

Panicking, I try to scramble on the wall of sand that I just erected. After I beat away a block, creating a small staircase, I manage to climb onto it.

That gives me an idea. I remove the lowest sand block. Although my arms are too short to reach it, removing it is surprisingly easy. All I have to do is *want* it to disappear. It doesn't pop into my mind, however. Instead it turns into a smaller cube that hovers above the ground, slowly revolving around its vertical axis.

I've got no time to wonder about it. The green guys can't reach me now, but the skeletons are still shooting their arrows at me.

I try to hop and materialize a sand block under my stick legs at the same time. It's a bit like skipping rope, something I was never good at as a child. But it works: The block appears, supporting my weight. I'm now standing on a column of sand three blocks high.

The green guys are clustering around the foot of the column, moaning in frustration. But before I even have time to gloat, I get another electrical shock from an arrow. I suddenly feel very weak. Another hit, and I'm finished.

I jump up and down a couple of times, materializing blocks below me. In this way I build a column of sand twelve blocks high, out of reach of the skeleton bows.

As I look down, I get dizzy. Far below me, an angry mob has gathered. I hear outraged *unnghs* and the rattling of bones. I better not make a wrong move! If I fall from the column ...

14

Without moving, I look around me. From up here, I have an excellent view of my surroundings. There's a distant island in the sea. Behind the mountains I discover a soft light that looks inviting.

What could that be? From up here, I can't say.

I stand on top of the pillar of sand like a bronze statue. I can't sit, but on the other hand, standing doesn't seem to tire my legs at all.

The effects of the attacks seem to lessen as I feel my strength return. But at the same time I feel something in my guts that's familiar and strange at the same time. It takes a while to identify it: I'm hungry.

While I stand there, a picture rises out of the depths of my memory. It definitely isn't from the Cubeworld. It's a face, quite a beautiful one. But the mouth is warped, the lower lip trembling. The mascara is smudged, the cheeks glistening with tears.

"Amely."

I have spoken the name loudly. I can't say it crossed my lips, because as far as I know, I don't have any. But I can still speak. Just for trial, I say it again: "Amely!"

I feel a dull pain throbbing deep inside me, very different from the sharp shocks that the monsters had dealt. The sadness of that face hurts, although I don't even know who she is. As hard as I try to remember more about her, only a white fog fills my memory.

The moon is moving slowly across the sky. The monsters down below still gather around the pillar. I'm beginning to wonder how I'll ever get safely down.

The problem solves itself, at least in part, when finally the sun rises. The desert is filled with orange, then yellow light. At that moment, the green guys and the skeletons burst into flames. I can hear their desperate *unnghs* and clicks, and I feel sorry for them. Well, almost.

As the sun rises higher, they disappear, until nothing is left but two walking cucumbers. They stand motionless beside the column and stare up at me. In contrast to the other monsters, they don't make a sound. They appear relatively friendly, if somewhat sad, but I don't trust them.

On the other hand, I can't stay up here forever. I think about jumping down, but then refrain from it. I still don't know much about the strange physics of this world, but the idea of falling down from this height is not very appealing, probably for a good reason.

Instead, I try to gather the block of sand right below me into my mind by punching it. It works. By removing block by block, I shorten the column until I'm standing right above the cucumber men. They look up at me disapprovingly. Around them, there's rotten flesh, arrows, and bones scattered all over the sand - apparently the remains of the other monsters.

What now?

I gather all my courage and jump. A small hiss sounds behind me. It frightens me. I run as fast as my inflexible legs carry me. The hissing grows louder, then there's an incredibly loud bang. I feel a shock that drains almost all of my life force.

I turn around. At the spot where the column of sand was before, there's now an irregular hole in the ground. Small cubes of sand are hovering everywhere. The two cucumbers have disappeared. Apparently they exploded, creating a crater. In hindsight, I realize that the hissing sounded suspiciously like the fuse of a pack of dynamite from an old cartoon series.

While I'm trying to discern what a cartoon series really is, I cautiously approach the hole. There seems to be no danger. As I come near one of the hovering sand cubes, it pops into my mind. I gather some more of them, as well as two arrows and two pieces of rotten meat that create such a feeling of revulsion that I cast them out again immediately.

I look up at the sky. The sun has risen quite a bit. I better not stick around here too long.

I remember the glow that I saw from the top of the pillar. It's probably a good idea to find out what it is about. But in order to do that, I have to climb the mountains before me.

Mountaineering in this world is easier than I had imagined. I can only jump one block high at a time, but it's not hard. Most of the time, the slopes are formed by natural stairs. If not, I can easily create my own steps by simply beating the earth in front of me. Once I even try it with a stone block. It works as well, but it takes a lot longer to remove it, and when it finally disappears, it's gone for good – no small stone cube in my mind this time. More strangeness.

When I reach the top of the mountains, the sun has already fallen well below the zenith. But I'm rewarded for my climbing with a heartening sight: Behind grassy hills I see something that's definitely man-made – or box-man-made, to be precise. It's a small hut, made from blocks of wood, with a stepped wooden roof. It even has a real door, and a small window beside it.

Excited, I jump down the slope toward it.

As I reach the plain below, I see a pig that's hopping around, grunting happily. At exactly this moment, my stomach grumbles. No, my stomach doesn't really make a sound, and I'm not even sure I have a stomach – I've got to be careful using metaphors in this world. But I feel an immediate, powerful urge to eat.

The pig definitely looks edible.

While I was sitting on top of my column last night, the strength that the skeleton arrows drained from me returned. But then I got hungry. Since then, I haven't recovered from the weakness caused by the explosion. I still run on reserve, so to speak. A single skeleton arrow or a touch by green flesh could kill me. I sense a connection here. Only with a full belly can I heal. In order to survive I need to eat.

I watch the pig. It looks cute. Can I really bring myself to kill and devour it? And if so, how do I go about it?

I approach the animal. It touches me with its pink cubic nose, without dissolving into my mind. So I must get brutal if I want its meat.

I hit the pig with my arm. It squeals and runs away.

No, I can't do that. I'm not the killer type.

In the meantime, the landscape has turned red. The sun disappears hastily, as if it had an urgent appointment. Night descends on the plain. The pigs and cows grunt and moo in a relaxed way. They seem to be unafraid of monsters.

I'm not.

Not far away, a warm glow brightens the night – the wooden hut. I'll be safe there. I hope.

"Unngh!"

That came from the left. I turn that way and almost jump out of my skin as I see a cucumber bomb that has silently crept up from behind. It's already starting to hiss.

I turn tail and run toward the light as fast as I can. I don't bother to check whether the monsters are still chasing me. At least the cucumber has stopped hissing.

A clicking of bones from the right suggests there are more creatures of the night out there to get me. I briefly consider climbing on a column like last night, but I don't have enough time. So to avoid the skeleton, I take a turn to the left and then circle back toward the light.

I almost reach the hut when an electrical shock hits me. The stupid skeleton has finally got me! That's my last thought before the lights go out.

3.

Something's wrong, but I don't know what.

I don't even know how I know that there's something wrong. It's just a strange feeling that the world isn't quite like it should be.

The world is a beach, with some terrace-like hills behind it. Waves wash silently against the sand. A cool breeze comes in from the sea. The air smells of salt.

The fact that everything around me is made of cubes feels strange, although I don't really know why. Nothing is as it should be, but it still feels familiar. It's okay to be here.

I wander among cube trees, climb steps up a hill, encountering a box sheep, and finally reach the top of the hill. There's a desert and a mountain range. I learn about the strange physics of this world, get attacked by monsters, save myself on top of a column of sand. I remember a sad face and realize that it's somehow not okay to be here after all. But I have no idea who this Amely is or what I can do to dry her tears.

The monsters below me burn in the morning sun, apart from two rectangular cucumbers that appear harmless enough.

I jump down onto the sand. The cucumbers start hissing. I'm scared and try to make my getaway.

I'm not fast enough.

4.

Something's wrong, but I don't know what.

Beach, box sheep, desert, sunset, monster, a column of sand, a light in the distance. Memories of a sad face. The sun burns monsters, only two remaining. A jump, an explosion, I barely get away. Hunger. Mountaineering. A pig that's too cute to eat. A chase in the dark.

The hut is very close. I reach the door, touching it. It opens. I get through and slam it shut behind me.

I did it!

I can hear the disappointed *unnghs* of the green guys that appear to be some kind of zombies. Through the window by the door I can see the surly face of a killer cucumber. It should be able to see me as well. All it has to do is explode, and I'm done. I'm sure that the wooden walls could not withstand the force of the detonation, let alone the window. But as if there is some kind of rule even suicidal monsters have to obey, it does nothing of the kind. It just stands there silently, staring at me.

Creepy.

The hut measures four by four cubes. On each side, there's a square window. Torches attached to the walls cast a flickering light. Like the walls, the floor is made of wood.

The only furniture is a roughly built stove made of stone, a strange boxlike table, and a large chest. There are no chairs, but they'd be useless anyway for people without knees.

Three panels of wood are attached to one of the walls, painted with black letters. The letters of the first one read: "You need a pickaxe and a sword." The second one holds the words: "Build a bed and sleep in it." The text on the third one I find the hardest to comprehend: "The exit lies in the Nether. Save Amely. M."

I ignore the distressed sounds of the monsters outside as I think about the messages. They tell me a couple of things: The writer obviously has a strange sense of humor, because this isn't really helpful. He seems to know Amely. His name begins with an *M*. Just great!

At least he has created the hut, exactly the thing I need right now. He probably knew that I would be coming this way. Or at least he knew that somebody would come to whom the name Amely meant something.

But what are those ridiculous tips for? What the cubic hell am I supposed to do with a pickaxe? Given the hungry mob outside, a sword might indeed be useful, but even armed, I doubt that I could accomplish much against them. And why would I need a bed? I'm not even tired!

Again, a flash of memory: some kind of seminar. I think I'm trained to be a youth group leader or something. The trainer, a guy trying to hide his young age behind a full beard, tells us we're in a plane that has crashed in a desert. He reads a list of things we can take from the burning wreck: a parachute, a few bottles of water, a flare gun, salt tablets, matches, a map of the area, a compass, a makeup mirror, and all kinds of other useless stuff. For some reason, we can only save five items and we're supposed to decide which.

I remember that my group quickly decided that the parachute was totally useless, since we were already on the ground. But then we were told that some experts on desert survival rate it as being useful as protection against the sun and as an optical signal to a rescue team.

A bed wasn't on the list of things that experts find

helpful for survival in a desert. A pickaxe and sword weren't on it as well.

And what is a Nether? Somehow, the word makes me feel uneasy, but I don't know at all what it means.

At least it says here that there's some kind of exit. That sounds encouraging. Maybe it leads me to this Amely, so I can save her, or at least comfort her. That seems to be a worthwhile cause!

So, now I have a goal. Unfortunately, I haven't the slightest idea how to get there.

Curious, I open the chest. That's another strange experience in this world full of weirdness. I don't look into the chest. Instead, its contents appear directly in my mind, separated from the things I already have there (which are some blocks of sand and earth, two arrows, and an egg).

The chest contains eight loaves of bread, a few seeds of something like grass, and a wooden cube. I gather everything in my mind and close the chest.

In order to eat the bread, all I have to do is think of it, and one of the loaves appears at the end of my arm. I lift it to my mouth. There's a strange crunching sound, the bread disappears, and I feel a little less hungry. I didn't even have to gulp it down, but I have a taste of fresh bread in my mouth. Or am I just imagining it?

I'm still hungry, so I eat another two loaves, until I get the feeling that my food storage is filled to the limit. Slowly, my strength returns.

So far, so good, but there are still monsters outside. I better wait for the morning.

I spend the time examining the wooden cube and the strange table. That's how I learn a few interesting things about the Cubeworld.

When I look at the wood with my inner eye, it seems there's something inside it. Not like inside a chest. It's more like there is the *possibility* within the wood to be something different. Wooden planks, for example.

As soon as I think that, the cube turns into four hollow cubes made of planks. But even those have the potential to be something different. I imagine two of them, one stacked on top of the other. Unexpectedly, instead of two boxes, I have four sticks of wood.

Energy can neither be created nor destroyed – I'm sure I learned that sometime – and since Einstein found that energy and mass are equivalent, the same should be true for matter. But in this world, Einstein obviously has no power. The mass of the sticks is much lower than that of the boxes, but the Cubeworld doesn't seem to care. But why should that be surprising, given that in this world, matter can be transformed into thoughts, as well as the other way round?

Here, matter and thought seem to be equivalent. A fascinating idea with a whole lot of interesting philosophical consequences. But I'm more the practical kind of guy.

As I approach the cubic table, a new window appears in my mind. I recognize it to be some kind of workbench, only I don't need any tools to work with it. Instead, I can use it to combine the things in my mind in new ways. After some experimenting, I discover that I can put two wooden boxes on top of a stick and – voilà – I get a wooden sword.

I'm extremely proud. Still, I suppress the urge to storm out the door and show the mob outside who's the boss. The thing in my hand looks too much like a toy for my taste. It doesn't even have a real edge.

I'd like to craft a little more, but I'm out of materials. All that's left of the wooden cube are three sticks, which apparently can't be turned into anything useful. Of course, I could try to tear some blocks from the wooden floor – if I understand the laws of cube physics correctly, that should make some nice wooden planks appear in my mind. But I've never been a vandal.

While I wait for the daybreak, I think about the third sign: The exit lies in the Nether. Sounds like something that exists deep down somewhere. But how can I get there?

Maybe I can ask the builder of the hut what it means. All I have to do is find him.

I shudder, thinking that he might be somewhere out there right now, chased by monsters. Maybe, by leading the mob of monsters to his refuge, I have cut off his only path to safety. He'll probably not be very happy about it, if he makes it here. On the other hand, he seems to know a lot about this world. If he's out there at night, it's his own fault, isn't it?

I peer outside into the darkness. The monsters still make frustrated *unnghs* and clicks, as if they can't understand how I disappeared so suddenly. They don't seem to be very bright.

Finally, the sun rises, and shortly after that, some living torches run around the house until they vanish, leaving rotten flesh and arrows. But where are the murderous cucumbers? Those guys are really sneaky, being so silent and immune to sunlight.

Cautiously, I open the door and look around. The coast seems to be clear.

The hut sits on a flat hilltop. Below me, there's a wide plain filled with box cows and cube pigs. In the distance, a forest looms. There is no sign of any human settlement. Whoever built the hut is nowhere to be seen. I'd like to thank him for creating the refuge I survived the night in. And I'd have a few questions to ask.

There are some trees growing around the hut. Wood! Now all I need is a way to get at it.

I envision the sword at the end of my arm and start flailing it at one trunk. I manage to chop a block of wood out of it, although the sword seems to take some damage in the process. The upper part of the tree doesn't fall down, like any decent tree should. Instead, it hovers in the air, as if an invisible force fills up the gap in its stem.

I don't stop to wonder about it but continue hacking at the trunk. After I have gathered four blocks of wood in this way, there's an ugly cracking noise and the sword vanishes. Seems like I destroyed it with my lumbering.

It doesn't matter. I know have enough wood to create a new one. Proud of myself, I enter the hut and turn the blocks into planks and sticks.

The first thing I make is another sword. Then I try to create a pickaxe. While trying, I discover a new combination of planks and sticks that gives me an axe. I continue experimenting, increasing my understanding of the weird logic of this world. Soon my mind holds a pickaxe, as well as two pieces of a wooden fence!

Since my supply of wood is almost used up, I go out again. Happy with my achievements, I'd like to whistle a tune, but that's difficult without lips.

Although the axe is made of wood, it cuts through the tree trunk as if it were butter. It's much quicker to harvest wooden blocks this way, and the axe seems to last far longer than the sword.

I'm so absorbed in my lumbering that I hardly register the soft hissing sound behind me. At the last moment, I turn around and stare into the surly face of a killer cucumber.

5.

Panicking, I try to hop away, but I don't get far when the thing explodes. I feel a strong electrical shock, and all strength drains from my body. At the point where the hut stood a moment before, there's a square crater with a lot of cubes of wood and earth hovering in it.

Oh boy! The builder of the hut will have a fit!

I consider repairing the hut, when another one of the murderous vegetables tries to sneak up from behind. Those things are really wicked!

This time, I react quickly enough to make my getaway. I race across the plain. The box cows ignore me.

After some time, I stop and look behind me. The monster is nowhere to be seen. Apparently, I have escaped.

I feel weak and hungry. Luckily, I still have five loaves of bread. I eat three of them. Slowly, I regain my strength.

What now? The sun is already sinking with uncanny speed. The hut is destroyed, and I don't dare going back there.

Should I spend another night on a pillar? That's not a very attractive prospect. What if I'm surrounded by cucumbers in the morning?

I know enough of the laws of this world by now to build a primitive shelter out of planks and cubes of earth. I finish it just as the sun sets.

As I close the last hole in the wall, it gets pitch-dark.

Not good.

I don't know enough about monsters, but I have a feeling that they're attracted by darkness. Maybe they can even materialize out of thin air. If one of them appears in my shelter, I'm a goner! Besides, in complete darkness, I won't even know when the night's over.

I seem to be in a hopeless situation.

After some thinking, I decide to make a hole in the ceiling. This doesn't cast very much light, but at least I can watch the stars move slowly across the sky.

Soon, I hear familiar *unnghs* and clicking noises outside. Luckily, no monsters appear inside. But suddenly, the hole in the roof is covered by another being. It has eight legs and two red, glowing eyes – and it's the size of a German shepherd.

Usually, I panic when I see a spider the size of my thumbnail!

The monster makes strange noises that sound like the last rattle of a strangled bird. The only comfort is that it's too large to fit through the hole. But I'm afraid that, unlike the zombies and skeletons, it will be unaffected by daylight. And I'd rather not meet this brute even in brightest sunshine!

By poking my sword through the hole, I try to make the monstrous spider go away. That seems to hurt it. It makes angry noises and jumps around, but it can't reach me. Again and again, I thrust my sword at it, until it disintegrates with a rattling noise. Unexpectedly, something drops down through the hole: two short lengths of rope! What on earth does a spider need a rope for? Weird, but no weirder than many other things I've seen in this world. I quickly gather up the rope, as I'm sure it will come in handy sometime in the future.

The stars continue to wander across the sky. Fortunately, the nights are as brief as the days. Soon the sky takes on a soft pink color that brightens quickly. The desperate *unnghs* and clicks outside tell me that the monsters are being burnt by the first sunlight.

But what about the cucumbers? They make no noise. For all I know, there might be dozens of them gathered around my house, waiting for me to open a gap in the wall.

I get an idea. With their small cubic legs, they can't climb, can they? I widen the hole in the ceiling, then build a short staircase and climb onto the roof. From up here, I can safely inspect my surroundings.

With a sinking feeling, I count no less than four killer cucumbers and three spiders sneaking through the grass around me. They seem to be unaware of my presence up here, but they will notice me as soon as I leave the house, I'm quite sure.

I'm trapped.

Of course, I could just stay where I am, in relative safety, hoping that the monsters will go away on their own. But I already feel hungry again, and I have only two loaves of bread left, which I'd rather save for later.

What now? I can't leave, but there's nothing to eat in here. To make things worse, I have this nagging feeling in the back of my mind that I'm running out of time, that something terrible will happen soon if I don't prevent it. I have no idea what that could be, but the thought makes me nervous.

I remember the messages that the unknown builder of the hut left for me: You need a pickaxe and a sword. Build a bed and sleep in it. The exit is in the Nether. Save Amely.

The last message is connected to the vague feeling of danger. But since I neither have any idea what the Nether is nor know the name Amely, this doesn't help me much. I already have a pickaxe and a sword. But where could I get a bed? And why is that important enough that somebody has written it on a sign?

I start experimenting in my mind with the wood that I cut before the cucumber drove me away – seven cubes, no less. Many planks and sticks can be made from it, but in my mind, I seem to be able to hold only very simple combinations. I need a workbench like the one in the hut.

Luckily, I discover how to make one quite quickly: Just four planks, grouped in a square. No sooner have I formed that picture in my mind than the bench appears before me.

Now I have many more possibilities. Randomly, I try combinations of sticks and planks. After some time, I have created a door, two trapdoors, a kind of hoe, and a large chest, but no bed. Obviously, something's missing. A bed needs a mattress, a pillow, and a blanket, doesn't it? But where can I get those?

I gather all my courage and make a hole into the wall, two blocks high. Before the cucumbers realize it, I set in the door. I can open and close it with a touch of my arm, like the one in the hut. Additionally, it has a window, through which I can now watch my surroundings.

My supply of wood is almost used up – only a few sticks and three planks are left. I consider the other items that I carry around in my mind. Maybe I can use other materials as well?

Blocks of sand and earth seem to be unsuitable for my purposes. Even my attempts to create something tasty out of the egg amount to nothing. I'm about to quit my experiments when I manage to combine some sticks with the rope in such a way that I get a fishing rod, complete with a metal hook. Now I only need a fishpond, and my worries concerning nutrition are over.

Unfortunately, I'm still in my crude house, watching the sun sneak down toward the horizon.

The thought of another night full of creepy noises and giant spiders makes me shudder. Quickly, I close the roof with some cubes of earth. A little light shines through the window in the door, but I still feel uneasy about the darkness inside. If I could only make some light!

I remember the torches attached to the walls of the hut. There was a stove as well. If I'm right about the ways of the world, all these things can be made of the materials you can find here.

The stove was made of stone. *You need a pickaxe and a sword.*

I start digging up the floor of my house with my bare arms, unearthing a layer of stone. Although the pickaxe is made of nothing but wood, I have no problems at all using it to cut neat stone cubes from the layer.

Soon I have dug a pit of considerable size, four cubes deep. I hold a dozen stone cubes in my head. I build a staircase of earth blocks and climb up to my workbench. With a little trial and error, I manage to build a stove.

As I place it on the ground and put a stick in the opening that's obviously meant to hold fuel, it lights as if by magic. A warm glow fills the hut.

Unfortunately, the stick doesn't last long. The darkness that fills the room after the fire dies down seems even deeper and more menacing than before. I need more wood!

It's now completely dark outside, and the monsters announce their presence with sinister noises. I look at the pit with unease. Quickly, I close it up with stones and soil.

The night passes slowly. There is an overwhelming feeling that while sitting around here waiting, I'm losing precious time. But nothing in the world could make me open the door and go out right now!

The zombies appear to be especially hungry tonight. Or maybe that's just my imagination, because I feel that I'm getting weak from hunger myself. I finish the last remaining loaves of bread and feel a little better. Still, I begin to realize that I'm in serious trouble.

As the day breaks, I've come up with a decision. Monsters or not, I need wood!

After the zombies and skeletons have burnt up, I peer out of the window in the door. No cucumbers in sight. I open the door and cautiously step outside, the puny wooden sword raised high.

I hear a rasping sound behind me and turn around. On the roof of my house is a giant spider staring at me.

Terrified, I turn tail, almost bumping into a killer cucumber that has crept up from the left, hissing in indignation.

I run for my life. And against all odds, I make a getaway! Apparently, these monsters give up on chasing me rather quickly. I can see them lurking around the hut, waiting for me to come back.

I run to the woods and hack at the trees as if my life depends on it, which it does. Once in a while, I stop and look around for cucumbers, but there are none.

When my axe finally breaks, I have gathered a significant amount of wood. If only the days weren't so damn short! The sun's already not far from the horizon. I can watch it sinking.

I think about going back to my hut, than disregard the idea. I can simply build another hut right here!

This time, I use the flank of a hill as a back wall and

manage to build a roof above me before nightfall. Making planks and sticks out of the wooden blocks, then building a new workbench and even another stove is almost effortless. I make enough sticks to fuel the oven throughout the night.

In this way, I spend the fifth night in the Cubeworld. But the next morning, I feel weak from hunger.

6.

The cows and pigs outside don't look cute anymore. They look positively tasty. Under the right circumstances, man turns into an animal.

They're not afraid of me. I can approach them, sword drawn, without them running away. If I had hands, I could pat them on their backs. That doesn't make it any easier. But I'm so desperate that I ignore my scruples and strike out.

My selected prey, a box pig, doesn't do me the favor of just dropping down dead. Instead, it squeals and runs away. I pursue it, feeling like a killer cucumber chasing an innocent traveler.

The pig tries to flee into the woods. Just as it reaches the trees, I manage to hit it a second time, then again. It squeals again, then it plops out of existence. It leaves two pork chops hovering over the grass. At least I don't have to butcher the carcass.

I take the meat into my mind. I could eat it raw, but I feel a strong reluctance at the thought. Shouldn't it be possible to cook it?

I go back to the hut. The stove has an opening where one pork chop fits in nicely. I feed it with a few sticks. Shortly thereafter, the mouthwatering smell of roasted pork fills the room.

My breakfast is cooked within a minute that feels like half an hour. I take it out of the stove and devour it. It tastes excellent. I cook the second pork chop and eat it as well.

Well fed, my confidence returns. I finally seem to have gotten the hang of this world.

However, I still have no idea what the Nether is. I can't even make a bed. And apart from the stove, I don't have any source of light.

I go out chopping wood.

The experience with the meat tells me that the stove is not only a source of light and heat. I try putting all kinds of things into it: the egg, an earth cube, the seeds, my sword, the fishing rod. However, there are no useful results until I put a block of wood in the upper compartment. To my amazement, the wood turns into coal.

I can use the coal as fuel. It lasts a lot longer than the sticks. Can it serve other purposes as well?

I carbonize another block of wood and systematically try out what happens if I combine the coal with other materials.

The second try leads to a spectacular success: As I combine the piece of coal with a stick, four burning torches appear in my mind. I can attach them to the walls just by wanting to put them there. Soon, flickering torchlight fills my pitiful hut, making it much cozier.

I'm incredibly proud of myself. If only I didn't have the feeling that time's running out ...

A spectacular sunset casts orange light across the landscape. Watching it through the window of my door, I realize for the first time how beautiful the Cubeworld can be.

What now? Just sitting around and waiting for dawn? Although I haven't slept for five nights, I'm not tired. I don't even know if I can sleep at all. I haven't even figured out how to close my eyes.

I look at the floor of my hut, covered with grass. Below it, there seems to be nothing but earth and stone. On the other hand, it's easy to dig down there. Maybe somewhere down below, there's more to discover.

I regard the pickaxe in my mind. It doesn't seem to be in very good shape. I better make a new one.

While I go about it, I get an idea. What if I use stone blocks instead of the planks? In a moment, I have a stone pickaxe that looks much stronger than the wooden one. I try it and discover that it cuts through the stone much faster. Before I know it, I have created a pit three blocks wide and deep.

So far, I haven't discovered anything but dirt and stone. But I'm instantly sure that there must be more, that somewhere below my feet there are untold riches to be found.

I get quite excited at the thought of treasure hunting. I chop at stone blocks like a madman. Soon the pit is eight blocks deep. But now I realize I have a problem: The deeper I dig, the darker it gets. The light of the torches obviously reaches down only so far.

The walls of the pit are too steep to climb. In my haste I forgot to leave a way up. But that's no problem, since my mind is full of stone blocks. I consider building a staircase, but that would take some time. Instead, I just materialize blocks below me, like I did in the desert. Just eight hops and I'm at ground level, as if using a lift. I've invented the cube elevator!

I create four torches, then remove the blocks below me. Out of exuberance, I don't stop at the bottom of the pit, but continue down, chopping away stone blocks beneath my feet. Slowly, I sink into a narrow shaft. Now there's only a small rectangle of light far above me. But I'm not afraid of the darkness any more. I can always move up again by placing the blocks below me that I've just gathered. Besides, the shaft is too narrow for monsters to appear.

As I dig deeper, I make an amazing discovery: Instead of another stone block, a piece of coal appears in my mind! Where did that come from?

I fix a torch at the wall of the shaft above me. Now I can see that the stone around me is riddled with black lumps. I've found a seam of coal!

Enthusiastically, I chop at the walls of the shaft until I have gathered a significant amount of coal. I'm now standing in a small cave.

I consider going back up with my load. I'm not sure whether it's night or day outside. But I'm in a miner's mood right now. Why not dig a little deeper? Maybe I can find other things. Wouldn't it be nice if I could dig up some gold?

I remove the block of stone below me. The next moment, I know that was a pretty bad idea.

There is nothing but deep darkness below me. Flapping my arms helplessly, I plunge down.

There's a splash and I'm covered by water. A strong current carries me away. I'm running out of oxygen quickly. Thrashing madly with my arms and legs, I manage to get my head above the water, gasping for air. The next moment, I'm pulled over a cliff, plunging down in a waterfall.

After some time, I'm able to pull myself out of the water. Pitch darkness surrounds me. I seem to be in some kind of underground cave, the size of which I can only guess.

Somewhere near, I hear a delighted *unngh*.

7

Oh boy! Just when matters were starting to improve ... Why the heck do such things always happen to me?

A voice rises out of the depths of my memory: "Pride comes before a fall."

It's the voice of my mother. I suddenly remember my mother's face, how tenderly she would gaze at me -- and how quickly her expression could change into a thunderstorm.

A twinge of longing cuts through me. I'd probably cry, if I knew how.

I need to get out of here!

"Unngh!"

I run blindly into the darkness, trying to put as much distance between me and the noise as possible. Suddenly, there's a hiss right before me. Oh no! I cut left and bang into a rock wall. A second later I feel the shock of the explosion.

Dazed, I grope around me. I'm still alive, but barely so.

"Unngh!"

Damn! What can I do? I blindly slash out with my wooden sword.

"Unngh!"

I try to pull together the last remnants of my wits. I need to see something. I need light!

I concentrate on my inner self. To my astonishment, I discover three burning torches. What an idiot I am!

Quickly, I attach one of them to the wall behind me. The cave is filled with flickering light.

It is larger than I had expected, the ceiling at least ten blocks high. To the left, there's a cliff, with a waterfall pouring down from it. Right in front of me, there's a cliff two blocks deep. Beyond it, a small river runs through the length of the cave until it becomes shrouded in darkness.

"*Unngh!*"

Near the riverbank is a zombie, looking up at me with murder in his eyes. He's jumping up and down, trying to get at me, but I'm two blocks above him. Had I made just one wrong step in the darkness ...

I hit the monster on the head with my sword. After a few strikes, he pops like a bubble, leaving behind a piece of meat with an expiration date that's probably a few years past.

There's no time to gloat, because at this moment, more *unngh*s sound from the dark parts of the cave. If they get me, I'm finished.

To make matters worse, I can now hear the clicking that announces skeleton bowmen. A single arrow will be more than enough to put me out of my misery. Whatever will happen then, I'm not eager to find out.

I desperately try to think of what to do. Running away won't work, because the only direction I can run is along the river to the right, where the monsters have been coming from. There's no time to consider other options, since a skeleton appears out of the darkness. It raises its bow and shoots. I barely dodge the bone arrow.

If only I had something to hide behind ...

The realization flashes through my mind: I have everything I need within me!

Quickly, I materialize two blocks of stone before me, one above the other. Another two, and before any monsters can get at me, I have walled myself in.

"See how you get at me now, you ugly brutes!" I yell.

"*Unngh!*" the zombies answer. They sound a bit smug.

I realize that walling myself in might not be a sustainable strategy for solving my problems. I'm on my last legs. To top it off, I'm getting hungry again.

I take an inventory of my mind. Between a lot of stone blocks and all kinds of trash, I discover my fishing rod. Might there be fish in the river running through the cave? But how am I supposed to fish, with all the monsters out there?

I brood for a while. Finally, I come up with a plan – or at least something remotely similar to one.

The first part is the most risky: I need to dig down right below me. I hesitate. What if I fall down into another cave? What if this time I'm not lucky enough to land in water, but instead plunge down onto plain rock, or on top of a killer cucumber?

But I have no choice. I gather my courage and hack at the stone block below me. Under it, there's just more stone. I cut through the next block, still standing on solid ground. With a gasp of relief, I listen to the monsters rummaging around two blocks higher than I am now. They can't reach me, and if I don't do anything stupid, it will stay that way.

Since I'm now in the ground, instead of digging straight down, I can proceed at an angle. I cut away the two blocks before me and then one deeper. In this way I can see what the layer of blocks below me is made of, before stepping on it. Nothing but solid rock.

I repeat this a few times, creating a staircase, leading deeper below me, that's safe to follow. From above, I can still hear frustrated *unngh*s and clicks.

When I'm eight steps deep, I start digging straight ahead. If I'm not mistaken, I should be well below the riverbed by now. At regular intervals, I place torches at the wall – I've got enough wood and coal with me to create as much of them as I need.

After a few steps I discover a new kind of stone block in the wall to the left of me. It contains brownish lumps. I cut away the block, transforming it into a smaller cube in my mind that somehow feels quite heavy. This appears to be iron ore. There are only three more cubes of it to be found. Either I was exceptionally lucky when I found the coal, or iron is simply harder to find.

Unfortunately, neither coal nor iron will fill my stomach, and I'm still feeling very weak. So I continue to cut my way below the cave until, according to my calculations, I'm below the wall opposite from where I'd built the block wall.

Now I've got to move upward again. I consider digging straight up – going in that direction, I can't fall into nothingness, after all. But what if I miscalculated and come up right below the river? Or if something falls on top of my head, a zombie, for instance? I'd better be careful!

So I use the same staircase method. This turns out to be a good idea, as when I remove a block of stone right before me, it doesn't simply disappear but is replaced by a different block falling down from above. This one is made from grainy material, probably some kind of gravel.

As I remove it, another block of gravel falls down, and another one. But the amount of gravel is not infinite. After five blocks, nothing more comes down. Instead, there's a vertical shaft before me. To be safe, I close it with a stone block. I continue digging, turning the direction of my staircase by 90 degrees to the left, and then another 90 degrees, until I proceed back in the direction I came from.

After ten more steps, as I remove the block before me, I

see light. I have opened a window in the wall of the cave!

I'm now three blocks above the floor of the cave. On the far side of the river, a single torch is attached to the wall. A mob of zombies, skeletons, and a single cucumber scurries around the low, rectangular tower that I erected.

On this side of the river, the coast is clear. However, I prefer to be cautious. I close the hole in the wall and continue to build my staircase at a right angle to my original tunnel, following the direction of the wall. After four more steps, I create another opening.

As I expected, I'm now right below the ceiling of the cave.

Now comes the complicated part of my plan. I remove another block, creating an exit from the wall. But before me, there's a drop seven blocks down.

My box legs don't allow me to kneel. But I can bend my torso. Carefully, inch by inch, I lean forward, until I look down at the cave wall. There's a moment of dizziness, and I almost tip over. In the last instant, I manage to place a block below me, gluing it to the cave wall.

I step out on the block and repeat the risky maneuver. After four more steps, I stand right above the river on a bridge that would be any structural engineer's nightmare because it is attached to the wall on only one side. But I know from chopping wood that the physical laws of this world work in a different way. I could probably even remove the block behind me without falling down. But I don't dare try it out.

Now for the last part of my plan: I take out the fishing rod and throw the line.

The line whirs through the air and with a soft plop the hook sinks down into the water. The line even has a bobber floating attached to it, which suddenly gets pulled under. I jerk at the rod, and a fish comes flying right into my head.

I walk across the bridge back to the wall, where I create a small cave. For an experienced Cubeworld inhabitant like me, it's a piece of cake to create a workbench and a stove, fuel it with coal, and cook the fish.

It's delicious.

Already feeling my strength returning, I go back to the edge of the bridge and catch a few more fish. The monsters down below don't seem to be aware of my presence.

Just as I pull the fourth fish out of the river, I hear a voice, as if from a great distance: "Marco!"

Startled, I take a step backward.

8.

Splash!

It takes me a moment to realize that I've fallen from the bridge. I'm standing in the middle of the river. I can feel the current pulling at my legs, trying to draw me deeper into the darkness.

Where did that voice come from?

Marco. The name seems familiar. I've heard that voice before as well.

A happy *unngh* reminds me that I'm not alone. The monsters have spotted me.

I flee, following the river. The light from the torches on the bridge and wall doesn't reach very far. I don't have time to place any new torches.

Another arrow hits me. Unlike me, the skeletons apparently can see in the dark.

There's nothing I can do but rush blindly into the darkness.

Then I step into emptiness. Fortunately, it's only a small waterfall two blocks deep.

The *unngh*s and clicking sounds around me seem to increase. Arrows buzz past me. To make things worse, I can now hear the rasping sound of a giant spider. The monsters approach me from every direction.

Just as I'm about to give up hope, I see a faint shimmer of light before me. Or is it just my imagination?

Another arrow drains my life energy. One more, two at the most, and I'm dead. Desperately, I run toward the light.

Now I can see that the river bends around an edge of the wall. Behind it, the cave widens into an area at least fifty blocks across.

To my surprise, I see a fenced garden with trees, flowers, and a small patch of wheat beside the river. There's a building of stone at one end. A dozen torches at the cave wall and on the floor cast an inviting light.

I run to the building, pursued by a gang of hungry monsters.

Another arrow barely misses me as I reach the door of the house. It isn't locked. I jump inside, slamming the door shut behind me.

The room is larger than it appeared from the outside, being partly carved into the rock wall. There are torches on the walls and even a stone fireplace with a crackling fire in it.

On one wall, an oven, a workbench, and a chest are neatly lined up. On the opposite wall is a bed. There are even pictures hanging on the walls. One shows a killer cucumber, another a landscape of box trees.

The owner of the house isn't at home.

I open the chest, finding tons of useful things: cubes of wood, coal, bars of metal, bluish crystals, dozens of loaves of bread, and even some gold bars. There are also things I can't make any sense of - a large amount of reddish dust, for example.

I close the chest. I'm not a thief, after all. But maybe I can rest a little before I face the darkness outside.

The bed looks very inviting. I lie down. Before I fall asleep, I seem to hear a faint, regular beeping sound. But I'm too tired to think about it.

"Hey! Who are you? How did you get in here?"

I literally jump out of the bed. Images of a dream fade from my mind: a world full of soft, flowing shapes, a tear-streaked face. I try to hold on to them, but they slip away like mist in the morning sun.

A figure is standing before me, clad in a kind of knight's armor that is shining bright blue. His square face is partly covered by a red beard.

"Who are you?" the blue knight demands.

I think about it. "Marco ... I think."

"Marco, you think!" The knight snorts. "And how did you get in here?" He doesn't seem to be very happy. I probably wouldn't like to find a stranger sleeping in my bed, either.

"There were monsters outside. The door wasn't locked, so I thought ..."

"I'm not asking how you entered the house, stupid!" he snaps. "How did you get on my server?"

"What?"

"How come you don't have a name tag?"

"What?"

He regards me a moment. "Did Lewis send you? Is this some kind of joke?"

"What?"

"Can you say something besides 'What'?"

"Um ..."

"Wait, I'm afk for a moment."

"What?"

The knight freezes. Standing completely motionless, he stares at me as if paralyzed. Maybe I should grab a few things from the chest and run before he comes to his senses - he doesn't seem very friendly, after all. Then again, I don't dare steal from a knight, and I don't want to face the monsters right now. So I just wait.

After a while, he comes back to life. "Lewis says he's got nothing to do with you. So who the heck are you?"

"I'm ... not sure."

"You really don't know who you are?"

"I may have lost my mind. My memory, I mean. Maybe my name is Marco. You don't know a girl called Amely, do you?"

"Um, no. I still don't understand how you got on this server. It sure isn't open to the public, and the firewall's supposed to be 100 percent tight."

I'd like to shrug, but I can't move my shoulders.

This whole dialogue would be less disturbing if I didn't have the feeling that all those strange words have a meaning somewhere deep inside me. But however hard I try, I can't remember any of it.

"Do you know what the Nether is?" I ask.

"Of course. Everybody knows that."

"Well, I don't."

"You're telling me you're a newbie? A newbie who somehow hacked into a state-of-the-art secure server?"

I don't know what to answer to that.

"Can you at least tell me where you are right now?"

"I'm here, aren't I?"

"Gosh! In what city, I mean! Are you even in England?"

England ... that sounds far away. Very, very far. "I'm ... not sure."

The knight sighs. "Okay. I don't know where this leads to, but maybe it will get interesting. You don't mind if I record this?"

Once again, I don't know what he's talking about. But I don't feel like admitting it, so I just say no, I don't mind.

"All right. So, whoever is watching: You won't believe it. I'm not sure I'm believing it myself. But this Marco somehow got onto our secure server, apparently without

48

knowing what he's doing. Maybe we'll find out how he did it. Anyway, such are computer games: full of surprises."

I look around, but there's no one he could be talking to. Maybe the shining knight is just crazy? That would go a long way toward explaining his behavior.

"Do you want to tell the people out there something about yourself, Marco?"

I don't want to disappoint him, so I say, "My name is Marco, I think. I'm looking for a girl, who I believe I must help somehow. Her name is Amely, I think."

"I see. A classical quest: Hero loses memory, must save girl from the clutches of evil villain."

He doesn't take me seriously. Fair's fair: I don't take him seriously, either.

"What's your name?" I ask.

"I'm Hon..." He hesitates, then says, "No, just call me Simon for now, all right?"

"Can you help me get to the Nether, Sir Simon?"

He laughs. "Sir Simon! At least you got manners!"

"I thought ... I mean, with your sword and armor ..."

He looks at me for a moment. "Okay. Wait a minute."

He opens the chest, takes out some items, and gets busy on the workbench. A few minutes later, he throws a couple of things on the floor before me.

I take a step toward them and gather them up in my mind. They're parts of the same kind of shining armor he wears, complete with a sword of the same bluish crystal. I put the armor on, admiring my glittering arms and legs. "Thank you!"

"You're welcome, Sir Marco!" He giggles. "Listen, this is the deal: I've got to play an adventure map down here, some kind of ancient buried temple. This will be no sweat if we do it together. You don't know what a let's-play clip is, do you? Of course you don't. Anyway, if we've done that, I'll show you how to get to the Nether, okay?"

Thinking about the voice, I'd rather be on my way immediately. But Simon seems nice enough and knows his way around here, and I'll probably need all the help I can get. So I say, "Agreed."

I stretch out my arm to shake his hand before I realize that neither of us possesses any.

9

Together, we leave the house. A small group of monsters greets us. I'd rather run back to the hut and dig a tunnel below them, but Simon just runs straight at them. A few arrows hit him, but he seems not to mind. Pulling out his sword, he slashes rapidly at zombies, skeletons, and giant spiders. It's a delight to watch him. Even a killer cucumber is no match for him: As soon as it starts to hiss, he hits it until it just vanishes, dropping a small amount of black powder.

He turns to me. "What are you standing around for? You sure could have helped me!"

"I'm sorry ... I'm just not much of a fighter!"

"Nonsense. Just hit 'em. Everybody can do that!"

"But the killer cucumbers ..."

He stares at me, then guffaws. "Killer cucumbers!" He can't stop laughing. "Killer cucumbers! Oh boy, I like that!"

After he calms down, he explains to me that the green explosive guys are called creepers. They are among the most dangerous beings of the Cubeworld, because they are unharmed by sunlight and make no noise. But down in the Nether, there are worse things to be found.

What he tells me doesn't make the Nether a very attractive goal. But just as I wonder whether it's really worth the risk, I hear the voice, calling me from far away, "Marco! Oh, Marco!" followed by a soft sob.

"Amely?" I shout.

"What?" asks Simon.

"Didn't you hear that?"

"Hear what?"

"The voice."

"What voice?"

"It called 'Marco, oh Marco'!"

He looks at me quizzically. "I didn't hear anything."

"Strange."

"Strange, indeed. Come on now, we've got some ruins to explore!"

We walk through the darkness. Once in a while, we encounter a single zombie, skeleton, or spider, but with Simon at my side, I'm not afraid of them. One time I'm the one who cuts down a skeleton with three quick strokes. I'm quite proud of myself.

We follow the river until we come across a high wall made of moss-covered stones. It's obviously not natural. Before it, there's a strip of sand three blocks wide. It looks a bit out of place down in this cave.

"Let's look for some kind of opening mechanism," Simon suggests.

"Can't we just cut a hole into the wall?"

"That's cheating. We must obey the rules."

"What rules?"

"The rules of this adventure map. No digging. Otherwise it wouldn't be fun."

To me, Sir Simon doesn't quite look like the type who always adheres to rules. But I don't object. Instead, I search for something that looks like it might somehow open the wall.

I find a block in the wall that has a little cube of wood attached to it. It looks like it can be pressed down. "I think I found it!" I yell.

"Wait. Don't touch ..."

Too late.

After I press the button, there's a grinding noise below

me. Suddenly, the sand I stand upon drops. I try to save myself with a leap onto safer ground, but I miss.

Both Simon and I plunge down toward some reddish glow. It looks suspiciously like lava.

"You fool!" is the last thing I hear before I burst into flames.

10.

Something's wrong, but I don't know what.

I don't even know how I know that there's something wrong. It's just a strange feeling that the world isn't quite like it should be.

The world is a rectangular room, lit by torches on the walls. A cozy fire crackles in a fireplace. There's a stove on one wall, with a strange rectangular table and a chest next to it. Pictures on the walls show a strange green cucumber-like thing that somehow makes me nervous and a landscape full of rectangular trees.

Startled, I stare at my arms. Where are my hands? Where they should be, there are just rectangular stumps.

Rectangular. That's what bothers me. The world is rectangular, just like the guy who stands before me, a red beard seemingly painted on his cubic head.

"You idiot!" the guy says.

"What?"

"Oh no, not again! Stop playing the innocent!"

"What?"

The stranger raises his arm stumps in the air. "Boy! You frazzle me out!"

"Who ... are you?"

The rectangular guy stares at me. "You aren't an AI, are you?"

"What?"

"No, that's impossible. An AI would say things like 'I don't understand your input,' not just 'what' all the time." He shakes his head. "You're quite convincing, feigning amnesia. You almost got me."

"I beg your pardon?"

"What's your name?"

"I ... I'm not sure."

"Gosh! This is getting tedious! What the heck, I'll play along, just for the sake of the audience."

Simon, as he calls himself, tells me I somehow turned up on his server – that's apparently a slang word for stone house – which I shouldn't have been able to do. That I've told him my name is Marco, and I'm looking for a girl named Amely, whose voice I've heard a couple of times out there in the cave.

As he mentions the names, I get a strong sense of déjà vu, as if I've been here before. A picture of a tear-streaked face appears before my inner eye. Is that Amely? She's beautiful.

"Are you listening at all?" Simon asks.

"What?"

"I just said you told me this Amely is to be found in the Nether."

"What's a Nether?"

Simon sighs. Instead of answering, he walks to the chest, opens it, and looks inside. "I don't have any diamonds left. Iron will have to do." For some reason, there's a reproachful tone in his voice.

He putters around at the strange table for some time. Suddenly, his appearance changes: While he wore a light blue shirt and dark blue trousers before, he's now covered in armor made of a shiny gray metal.

A moment later, he drops some items on the floor. They seem to hover slightly above the ground. As I take a step forward to examine this strange phenomenon, the items disappear. Somehow, I can now feel them within me!

I'm baffled. What strange world have I gotten into?

"Put on the armor!" Simon commands.

It takes me a while to figure out what he wants me to do.

Sometime later, we're standing at a gap in the ground three blocks wide. Behind it, a moss-covered wall rises up. On the way here, I learned a lot about the creepers, zombies, skeletons, and giant spiders we came across. When we weren't fighting monsters, Simon told me about the Nether, a forbidding place that for some reason I wanted to visit before I did a really, really stupid thing and killed both Simon and myself in the lava pit down below.

Cautiously, I bend over the gap and look down. The thought of falling into that abyss makes me shudder.

"We should have hit the button with an arrow," Simon explains.

I nod my head, as if nothing could be more obvious.

"There's probably another button or lever somewhere that pulls out a drawbridge or something. Help me look for it. But don't you dare touch anything! Got it?"

Before I can answer, I hear a voice calling me, as if from a great distance, "Marco? Marco, can you hear me?"

"Yes, I hear you!" I shout at the top of my voice.

Apparently, it's not loud enough. "Oh, Marco!" the voice whispers, then starts sobbing.

"What's this about?" Simon asks.

"The voice ... it called me ... didn't you hear it?"

"Oh boy, what have I gotten myself into!" Simon exclaims.

I agree.

After some time, Simon finds a button on a block of stone near the gap. Ignoring his own advice, he presses it right away. As a result, some kind of bridge moves out of the stone wall, crossing the abyss. At its end, a large gate appears.

"There we go!" Simon says triumphantly. "All you have to do is press the right ..."

He's cut off by an arrow whirring close by his head. Out of the gate, a few dozen zombies, skeletons, and creepers storm toward us across the bridge. They scramble over one another to get to us, with some of them getting pushed off the bridge. At the same time, more skeletons appear at the top of the wall, targeting us.

"We need to fight our way across the bridge," Simon explains. I'm not an expert on sieges, but I could have guessed as much.

We hack at the monsters with our swords, scattering pieces of meat and bone. Simon seems to be talking to himself all the time: "Oh boy, that was close. What a nasty little sneaker. Wait, I'll show you! Ha, did you see that?"

Fortunately, the bridge is quite narrow, so we only have to fight one or two monsters at a time. If only the stupid skeleton bowmen weren't raining arrows down on us! Soon, my health level drops down close to zero.

"Retreat!" Simon yells. We turn tail and stop only after we're a safe distance away. The monsters lose interest in us pretty quickly and stay lurking in front of the ruins.

Simon drops an object that looks like a bulbous bottle. "Potion of healing," he says.

I pick up the bottle and empty it into my mouth. It tastes very bitter.

"Yuck!" I say, but at the same time I can feel my strength returning.

"What?" Simon asks.

"I said, 'Yuck,'" I explain. "This medicine tastes awful!"

"How would you know?"

I look at him quizzically. "I just tasted it, didn't I?"

He doesn't answer, but stares at me for some time.

Finally, we return to the battle, until the arrows nearly kill us again. But this time, we have practically decimated the monsters, with the help of one creeper who exploded right on the bridge, blowing half a dozen skeletons and zombies into the abyss.

In our third attempt we manage to cross the bridge. We enter a torchlit room five by five cubes in size. Here we are out of range from the skeleton arrows. However, I have the feeling that our difficulties are only just beginning.

"We made it," Simon comments. "But I guess our difficulties are only just beginning!"

At the end of the room, there's a metal door, without any apparent opening mechanism. Above it, a wooden sign reads, "Say the magic word."

Without thinking, I say, "Open up, please!"

Simon looks at me as if he wants to flip me the bird, if only he had an index finger. "Do you think this has speech recognition, or what?"

"I don't know about that," I reply, "but the door is open, isn't it?"

He turns around and stares. "How ... how did you do that?"

"Sometimes, a bit of courtesy takes you further than brute force," I reply smugly, stepping through the door. Behind it is a long passage. It's not lit by torches, but by glowing cubes set into the walls in regular intervals.

"That's glowstone," Simon explains. "You can find it only in the Nether."

"So we're in the Nether now?" I ask.

"No," he answers without bothering to explain the contradiction.

The passage leads to a dead end. There's a hole in the floor, filled with water.

"We need to go through this," Simon says.

"Through? What do you mean? What if there isn't any 'through'?"

"Don't be such a wimp. Worst case, you drown, awake in my bed, and don't remember anything."

"Does that ... does that mean I died before?"

"Once at least, with me at your side. You probably died a hundred times bef—" Simon stops himself. "Gosh, I'm already talking like you are real!"

I don't comment that.

"Come on now, jump into the hole!" Simon says.

"You first."

"Sissy!"

"Sissy yourself!"

He sighs. "All right. Watch your oxygen supply. If you feel you won't make it, come back here and get some air, okay?"

"Okay."

He looks at me with what I guess is indignation, then steps into the hole, sinking down quickly. I can see him going deeper, then vanishing in an opening in the shaft. After a moment, I seem to hear a distant "*Aaaaargh ...*"

Was that him, or some unknown kind of monster?

I wait for a moment. Simon doesn't reappear.

Maybe instead of jumping in the hole, I should go back to his house. If he died, he should be there now. In that case, I could save myself from a rather unpleasant experience and keep my memories.

On the other hand, I don't want Sir Simon the brave knight to call me a coward. So I gather all my courage and jump into the pool of water.

I immediately sink. Before I know it, I'm pulled by a strong current through an opening in the wall and down a narrow channel.

I can feel my supply of oxygen dwindling. But it's impossible to swim against the flow.

I feel my strength drain away. I'm desperate for air!

Just as I'm about to lose consciousness, I shoot out through an opening into a giant cave. Far below me, half of the floor is covered by a lake.

Tumbling down, I let out a desperate "*Aaaaargh ...*"

11.

With a loud splash, I fall into the lake. I struggle to the surface, then swim to the bank, where Simon is already waiting. He isn't looking at me, but instead stares beyond me. As I climb out of the water and turn around, I see why.

The cave is at least thirty blocks high. A large part of the ceiling is made of glowstone. A giant face is carved into the opposite wall. It's the face of a girl.

Her eyes are open. Waterfalls pour out of them, cascading over her cheeks into the lake. Her mouth is wide open, as if she were screaming.

"Amely!" I whisper.

Simon looks at me. "Now I get it!" he says. "You're part of this adventure map! Somehow, this mod has created a backdoor on our server. That's how you got in. I must admit that's pretty clever! And I thought a guy from Germany had designed this mod. You got me!"

I don't understand a word, but that doesn't matter. "We need to go through the mouth," I state.

"Of course," Simon agrees. "It's the only exit."

So we get on our way. In spite of our iron armor, we have no problem swimming across the lake. Below the face's chin a staircase leads up to the mouth.

As I climb onto the lower lip, which seems to consist of some red, soft material, there's a tremendous scream. A powerful force pushes both of us back into the lake.

"What the hell was that?" Simon calls.

"She screamed," I explain.

"You think?" Is that sarcasm in Simon's voice? "This time, we wait at the corners of her mouth for the scream to pass," he suggests.

"All right."

We do as he said, but there's no scream coming.

"Damn. The cry is probably triggered by a pressure plate in her mouth. You go ahead, I'll wait here. As soon as the scream is over, I'll go inside and try to disable the mechanism."

Courageously, I climb into the mouth, but there's no scream this time. Instead I hear a soft sob coming out of the darkness.

"I can't see anything," I exclaim.

"Wait, I'm coming." Simon attaches a torch to the wall inside the mouth. Now I can see a staircase leading down.

Together, we follow it. The staircase seems to have no end. Every few steps, Simon places a torch. After a while, he says, "Wait a minute!"

I turn around. "What is it?"

"This can't be!"

"What do you mean?"

"We're much too deep down."

I look at him blankly.

"The ground goes down only sixty-two blocks below sea level," he says as if that could explain anything. "We should have come across bedrock long since." As by now he's able to identify my uncomprehending look, he adds, "Bedrock is the stuff the bottom of the world is made of. Below that, there's literally nothing."

"But we're here," I observe. "We've obviously climbed deeper down than sixty-two steps."

"That's what I don't understand. I wouldn't have thought there's a mod that changes the game mechanics on such a deep level."

Wisely, I refrain from asking what that means.

We continue downstairs. The stairs really appear to have no end.

"Maybe this is a trick," Simon says.

"A trick?"

"Maybe we're teleported back upstairs every twenty steps or something. In that case, we could climb down till kingdom come. Wait, I'll check. I'll be back right away."

Before I can ask him how that can be if the stairs below us are not lighted by torches, he's gone.

After a long time, he comes back. "No, it's not a trick. I've counted the steps: one hundred and two."

"So we go on?"

"Yes. I want to know how deep this goes."

On step 152, Simon runs out of torches. "We need coal," he says.

I'm about to suggest that we put the rules where the sun never shines and hack our way through the stone when I hear the sobbing again. It seems to be really close.

"Did you hear that?"

"Hear what?"

"A sob. Seems to be close."

"This is getting creepy."

"I agree."

"Anyway, it's just a stupid game! Let's continue in the dark, shall we?"

"I'm not sure I like that idea."

"Sissy!"

"Sissy yourself!"

Indecisively, we stand on the staircase for a moment. Then Simon pushes me aside. "All right, I'll take the lead."

We continue downstairs until the last torch is nothing but a tiny point of light in the distance.

"The staircase ends here," Simon whispers.

This should be good news, but somehow I'm not reassured. At least on the stairs, there weren't any monsters.

We walk down a short corridor.

"Damn!" Simon shouts. "An enderman! Don't look into its eyes!"

"You mean those bright spots over there?"

They hover in the darkness, surrounded by a whirl of softly glowing spots of purple.

Hypnotized, I'm staring right into them. Something deeply evil emanates from them. It makes me feel sick.

A picture comes up from my memory.

"I ... I know these eyes!" I stammer.

"Don't look away!" Simon says. "As long as you look into its eyes, it won't move!"

I hear Simon's steps behind me. "Hey! Where you're going? Don't leave me alone with this thing!"

"Don't worry, I'll be back in a minute. As long as you don't look away, nothing will happen to you!"

Easier said than done. I try to stand up to that evil gaze. It makes my whole body shudder.

"What did she tell you?" a voice in my head asks.

I'm far away, in a brightly lit room. White walls, a desk with a computer on it, a couch covered with a length of paper.

He wears a white coat. The warm smile he showed when he asked me how he could help me is gone. His gray eyes penetrate me to the core.

I want to look away, but I mustn't.

Somewhere in my head there should be the words that I had carefully formulated before entering the room. But I can't find them. It's as if his gaze drains my will. "She ... she said that you ... mistreated her," I stammer.

"Mistreated" is not the word I wanted to say. "Abused," it should have been.

The doctor laughs out loud, as if I'd made a good joke. "You accuse me of mistreating Amely? My own daughter?"

"You're not her father!"

"I married her mother when she was seven years old," he says calmly. "I raised her like my own child, believe me. Even when I realized she's ... different."

His hand rests on my shoulder, like a monster's tentacle out of dark dreams. I want to push it away, but I'm unable to move.

"Amely suffers from paranoid schizophrenic disorder," he says in that gentle tone he probably uses when he tells patients how long they have left to live. "You know that that means?"

I can't bring out a word.

"Schizophrenia is much more common than most people think," he explains. "It's estimated that up to two people out of a hundred suffer from it. Paranoid schizophrenics have difficulty separating the outside world from their inner state of mind. For instance, they sometimes hear their own thoughts as if they were voices from the outside, or they think things they imagined really did happen to them. At times, they interpret accidental occurrences as something that has been planned with regard to them. That's why they often think the whole world is conspiring against them."

"Amely is not crazy!" I object.

He ignores me. "I diagnosed her condition when she was nine years old. We tried to enable her to live a normal life, sent her to a regular school. I prescribed her medication. It worked for a while. But in the last months, the hallucinations have come even more frequently. Maybe it's puberty that deteriorates her condition. Maybe she doesn't take her pills anymore. I'm afraid we can no longer let her go to your school."

I think of her, standing at the edge of the schoolyard, alone. She was always alone.

I tried to talk to her. She sent me away. But the more she rejected me, the more I felt that something was wrong. That she was carrying a load too heavy for a single human.

"Please go away," she said, over and over again.

I left her alone, never pushed too hard. But I came back again and again, trying to show her that she mattered to me. That I'd listen as soon as she was ready to open up.

Then, one day, she told me what she lived through.

"You're lying!" I say to Amely's stepfather, although there's doubt creeping in the back of my mind. What if all the awful things she told me about were nothing but hallucinations?

The mild, sympathetic expression on his face is pulled away like a curtain, revealing a cold, pitiless, harsh countenance. "You dare to come into my office under a pretense, accusing me!" His voice is calm, but threatening. "I don't have to put up with this! You're going to stay away from Amely from this moment on, got it? If you as much as ..."

A light flares, pulling me out of my memory. Simon has attached a torch to the wall. Its flickering light reveals a large rectangular room made of dark stone blocks.

The thing he calls an enderman unexpectedly appears right before me. It's huge, at least half again as large as I am. It has a slim rectangular body, completely black, with a cubic head and arms almost touching the floor. It hits me, sending a shock through my body.

"I told you not to look away!" Simon says. He pulls his sword and hacks at the enderman like a berserker. But the monster isn't fazed by it. It continues hitting me, draining my life energy almost completely.

I want to run, but the glowing eyes seem to nail me to the floor.

"You can't run from an enderman," Simon shouts. "So stay where you are and fight!"

I strike out with the sword weakly. Nevertheless, as I hit the enderman, it pops out of existence, leaving a green ball behind.

Simon examines it. "Look at that! An ender pearl! Not bad for a start!" He looks at me. "You don't look too well." He throws another potion of healing at me.

I don't move. The memories make my body convulse as if someone is hitting me in the stomach over and over again.

"Where ... am I?" I ask.

Simon sighs.

12.

"Don't tell me you lost your memory again!" my companion says.

"No. Quite the opposite. I remember something."

"Great. Has it anything to do with the game?"

"You think this is a game?"

"Anyway, why don't you drink a potion of healing and then we'll see what comes next. The enderman wasn't our last opponent, I'm sure."

The thought of encountering another being with such terrible eyes makes me shudder.

After I drink the potion, we search the room. Apparently, it has no other exit. We check every inch of the walls and floor, but there's no secret mechanism.

"Looks like a dead end," Simon states. "Now we have to climb the whole stupid staircase again. At least I can collect the torches on the way."

But as we leave the room, we're in for a surprise. The staircase has somehow vanished. Instead, what lies before us is a straight passage.

"Holy creeper!" Simon exclaims. "How did you manage to do that?"

"I didn't do anything."

"I mean whoever programmed this mod. This is unfair!"

The passage leads into another room that looks exactly like the one the enderman was in. But there's no monster inside. Instead, two beds stand side by side in the middle of the room.

Simon is not interested in the furniture, however. He inspects the walls. "Bedrock! Just like the other room."

I help him search the walls and floor, then the passage.

Again, we find nothing. Finally, we search the room where the enderman was a second time, to no avail.

"We're trapped!" Simon says.

"We still have our pickaxes," I point out.

"They're useless. Everything down here is made of bedrock, which is indestructible."

"So how do we get out of here?"

"We don't." Simon looks around as if to make sure nobody's watching. "So our little adventure comes to an unexpected end," he says. "I've never come across a mod like this before. Nothing works according to the rules. I wish I had some TNT. It wouldn't destroy the walls, but at least we could put an end to our misery in style."

He turns toward me. "Kill me!"

"What?"

"Kill me! That's the only way to get back to where we last slept. We obviously walked into a trap without any exit."

"But ..."

"Come on now! Just do it!" He points at my sword.

I hesitate. I've come to like Sir Simon. I don't want to lose my only friend in this strange world.

"You can stay down here if you like. But I can't just sit around here. I've got a clip to make. The viewers won't stick around watching us doing nothing. They want action!"

There has been more than enough action for my taste. I suddenly feel very tired. "Maybe we should rest a while. Those beds in the other room looked quite inviting, I think."

"Are you crazy? Once we sleep in them, if we die afterwards, we'll spawn in them. Then we'd be trapped for good. Are you going to hit me now, or what?"

"What about me? Who's going to kill me if you're gone?"

Simon thinks about it. "Good point. Do you have any cubes of stone or earth with you? Anything you could build a tower with and jump to your death?"

"No."

"That's too bad. Well, I guess I'll have to find a way to free you, then. There must be some kind of mechanism outside this trap."

"I don't want to stay here all alone. What if the torches burn out?"

Simon sighs. "Have you ever seen a torch burn out?"

"No," I admit.

"See, I'll leave you all the torches I have, together with any other stuff I carry. Just kill me, will you?"

"If you say so ..." I overcome my reluctance and hit Simon halfheartedly.

"Good! Go on!"

A few more hits, and he vanishes, leaving behind a large amount of objects hovering above the floor. I pick them up, amazed what a single mind can hold: lots of potions in various colors, Simon's sword and armor, tools, bars of metal, at least thirty loaves of bread, and a lot of other stuff.

While I wonder how to kill time until Simon rescues me, I hear a whisper: "Marco!"

Where did that come from? I follow the passage. As I enter the other room, I stop in my tracks.

There's someone lying on one of the beds. It's Simon.

As I walk toward him, he gets up, looking around as if in amazement.

"What the f ... Why am I here?"

That's a question I'd like to get answered as well.

"What a frigging stupid mess!" he shouts. "I'd like to

have a little discussion with the programmer of this mod! This is unfair!" He goes on swearing and complaining about the deviousness of a person he calls a programmer. Some kind of deity, maybe. As usual, I don't understand a word, but I don't dare interrupt him.

I give him back the things he dropped when I killed him. He pulls on his armor and we examine every block in the room another time. But to no avail.

Finally Simon raises his arms. "I don't know what to do! For some reason, I can't even get into creative mode anymore! This is no fun! What the hell are we supposed to do down here?"

"Sleep, maybe?" I suggest. It seems to be the only thing to do, and I still feel tired.

"Gosh, I think I already told you that ...," he says, but then interrupts himself. "Damn! You're right! Why didn't I get it before? Our spawn points were adjusted to these beds even before we arrived here. Maybe we get teleported somewhere else if we sleep in them a second time. Anyway, we've got nothing to lose. If you wake up in this room and I'm gone, wait a while, then go to sleep again, okay?"

"Okay," I say, although I haven't understood a word.

He lies down on one of the beds without bothering to take off his armor. I follow suit.

As soon as I lie down, I fall into a deep sleep.

I awake in bright light. My vision is blurred. I still lie in some kind of bed, but apparently it isn't the same I went to sleep in. Something's in my throat that doesn't belong there. I'd like to take it out, but I can't move my arms. I'm not even able to turn my head. It's as if I'm trapped within a body that doesn't belong to me.

Above me, there's some oval thing with dark spots. A

face? A bright light flares up, blinding me.

"Any reaction, doctor?" The voice seems familiar. But the word "doctor" makes me uneasy.

"Just the normal contraction of his pupils. A reflex, nothing more. His condition is unchanged, I'm afraid."

There's a soft moan – a small, miserable noise. A piece of hope just died.

I'm here, I want to shout. Don't you see me? But I begin to sink down into a dark shaft. Desperately, I try to cling to the vision, but I can't hold on to anything. The light shrinks until it is nothing more than a tiny spot.

"Help!" I cry. "Please, get me out of here! Don't leave me!"

"Stop shouting like this!"

I get up, instantly standing next to my bed.

Simon looks at me, his square face as expressionless as ever, but I can sense the distress in his voice. "Why are you making such a ruckus?"

"I'm ... sorry," I stammer, still shaken by the experience. "I ... had a bad dream." But was it really a dream? It seemed so real!

"You dreamed?" Simon asks, as if it were something indecent.

I don't answer. Instead, I walk straight to the wall and hammer at it with my arm stumps. I'm feeling like a prisoner sentenced for life, who realizes for the first time the hopelessness of his situation.

"Stop it!" Simon commands. "I already told you bedrock is indestructible!"

I stop. The fine crack that appeared in the block before me vanishes. I turn to him. "Are you sure?"

"Of course I'm sure," he says, but there's doubt in his

voice. He takes out a pickaxe and starts hacking at the wall. There's no effect at all.

"Strange," I say.

"There's nothing strange about it. Bedrock is indestructible, like I said. The whole idea is that designers of adventure maps have something that stops players from cheating."

"When I hammered at the wall, there was a small crack."

"Nonsense!"

"No, really. It vanished when I stopped. I'll show you!" I start beating at the wall, but nothing happens. "Odd. There was a crack before, I swear!"

"You imagined it."

"No, I didn't!"

"Yes, you did. There's no way out of here."

"What now, then?"

"I'm going to restart the server."

"What?"

"Forget it. We'll start all over again. You won't remember anything."

For some reason, I'm immediately scared. "Don't do that!"

"Why not?"

"I ... I don't want to lose my memory! I don't want to start all over again!"

"Do you have a better idea?"

I stare at the wall. I think about the cold eyes of the doctor, his false smile, Amely's tear-streaked face, the strange dream I had. I'm fed up with this nonsense!

I begin hammering at the wall. The more I beat at it, the angrier I get.

"I don't believe it!" Simon says.

I ignore him. I'm tired of his incomprehensible comments. I just want to get out of here!

I hear the laugh of the doctor in my head: "You accuse me of mistreating Amely? My own daughter?"

I want to beat the grin out of his face! I pull back, gathering strength, and hit the wall with all the power I have.

There's a loud cracking sound. Startled, I stop. A deep crack appears in the stone cube before me. It doesn't vanish when I stop beating at it. Instead, it starts to spread to the next cubes. Soon, a maze of cracks riddles the whole wall.

Then, with a sound like thunder, all the blocks shatter at once.

"Wow!" Simon exclaims, followed by a startled, "Oh boy!"

13.

The room behind the wall is the size of a ballroom, lit by a glowstone ceiling and dozens of torches on the walls. But there are no well-dressed couples waltzing across the dance floor to the tune of an orchestra. Instead, there's a cacophony of *unngh*s and clicks from dozens, if not hundreds of monsters – not counting the silent creepers and endermen.

"Back to the passage!" Simon yells. I run after him, past the beds. We take our stand at the entrance of the room, where it's easier to defend ourselves.

It's a gruesome battle. Side by side, Simon and I flail at the monster horde storming at us. A few times, I'm about to kick the bucket. If not for Simon's potions of healing, we'd never survive.

"Look at the floor!" he says.

I stare at the mess of pieces of meat, arrows, and bones at my feet. "Why? What's so interesting about it?"

"Nothing. But while you look at the floor, you can't meet an enderman's eyes!"

The endermen! I had completely forgotten about them. Cautiously, I glance across the floor until I see five pairs of slender black legs at the far end. In their dark suits, the endermen look like bored guests at a party.

"Don't look at them!" Simon whispers.

"Marco?" someone calls out.

Amely! She's there at the far end of the room. I must ...

At the last moment, I realize that this is a trap. Somehow the endermen must imitate her voice. It takes all my willpower to resist the urge to look up at them. "There isn't a girl standing with them, is there?" I ask Simon.

"No," he answers. "But maybe some of them are really endergirls. Want me to ask?"

"Very funny." Although that was supposed to be sarcastic and our situation is far from amusing, I burst out laughing. Simon joins in.

"We'll take them on one at a time," Simon suggests after we calm down. "I'll do it. You just keep your eyes on the floor, got it?"

"Okay."

The next moment, an enderman appears before us and starts hitting us with its long arms.

"What are you waiting for?" Simon yells. "You want me to do all the work myself, or what?"

"I thought I was supposed to look at the floor," I say in my defense, but I start hacking at the black foe.

As long as he's in front of us, I can't see the others. But as soon as he vanishes with another hit, I stare right into the eyes of one of his kind waiting calmly at the far end. Quickly, I avert my eyes, but that only draws him toward me. At the same moment, another one appears, apparently attracted by Simon.

"Shit!" my companion exclaims, as we continue our bloody task.

This time, it's a close shave. I'm as good as dead as my enemy continues to beat at me. He pulls back for another swing of his long arm, which will certainly put me out of my misery. I'm saved by Sir Simon, who has killed his opponent and comes to my rescue. He hits the enderman, who bursts like a bubble.

"Thanks!" I say, staring at the floor.

"You're welcome. Here, this is my last potion of healing."

Gratefully, I gulp down the bitter concoction. I've long since become used to the foul taste.

Simon draws the fourth enderman near. We've become a practiced team, so we hack it to pieces before it can deal much damage. The last of the sinister guys hasn't much of a chance, either.

"We've done it!" I say.

Simon, however, seems not so pleased. "My armor barely holds together, my sword's almost broken, and I don't have enough iron to create replacements. We won't survive another battle like this one."

"Maybe these were all of the monsters there are," I say, trying to comfort him. "As many of them as there were in that room, it's probably been some kind of storage."

"You haven't got a clue! There are infinite numbers of monsters. They emerge right out of the darkness or near magical cages called spawners. We're lucky there weren't any in the next room."

"Anyway, thank you. You saved my life!"

"And you saved mine." He stares at me for a moment. "By the way, how did you do that?"

"Do what?"

"Shatter the bedrock wall. As if you smashed a windowpane. I've never seen anything like it!"

"I don't know. I was simply ... angry."

Again, he stares at me for some time, but he leaves it at that.

We sift through the trash the monsters left, finding lots of arrows, five ender pearls, and the two beds, which somehow have shrunken to the size of toys during a creeper explosion.

"Strange," Simon says. "Normally, it's rare for an

enderman to drop a pearl. This time, every single enderman left one. I wonder what that means."

I'm not even trying to understand what he's talking about.

We walk across the large hall. At the far end is a wooden balcony, with a staircase leading up to it. Climbing the stairs, we discover a large chest a the top.

Simon opens it. But there's no treasure inside, just a small amount of yellowish power, smelling like sulfur.

"Blaze powder," Simon says. "I don't like this at all!"

"What's the matter? Is it dangerous?"

"No. Actually, blaze powder is quite valuable. You can create a lot of useful things with it."

"So why don't you like this?"

"Because you combine blaze powder with ender pearls to make ender eyes. They are used to locate fortresses, and to activate the end portal you can find in them. Those portals lead to the End."

"The End?"

"It's some kind of other dimension, like an island in the void. Not very large, but extremely unpleasant. Compared to the End, the Nether is a piece of cake."

"What's so bad about it?"

"You encounter the Enderdragon, the worst and most powerful creature of all. Once you go through an End portal, there's no way back. You either kill the dragon, or he kills you."

"And if you kill him?"

"Then you win."

"Win what?"

"You just win. Winning is what it's all about, isn't it?"

"You're worried about this blaze powder just because

you can use it to get to this End?"

"I'm worried because obviously we have to go there. For sure it's no coincidence that all the endermen dropped pearls, and we find a chest full of blaze powder in the same room. The designer of this mod intends us to go to the End."

I try to emanate confidence. "Sounds like a task for two heroes like us!"

"Sounds like a recipe for suicide to me."

We open the door to see a passage ten blocks long. At its end, a waterfall pours down from the ceiling.

I stare at it. "What's wrong with the water?" I ask.

"What's wrong with you?" Simon replies. "Haven't you seen a waterfall before?"

"Not one like this. Where does all the water go? There seems to be no drain. This passage should be completely under water within minutes."

"That's just how it is," Simon says. Strange: He's totally baffled that I can destroy a wall made of rock cubes, but seems completely unfazed by this phenomenon.

"Obviously, we have to go up there," he comments.

"Up where?"

"Up through the waterfall."

"How's that supposed to work?"

"Just follow my lead." He steps into the waterfall, then glides upward like riding an elevator.

I stare at the water for a while, until I hear a distant *aaaaargh* ...

I gather my courage and step into the water, which is pouring down on me. Not surprisingly, I'm not pulled upward. All that happens is that I run out of oxygen.

I step out of the water, gasping for air. Simon has

forgotten to mention some detail, I guess. What now?

I try it again. This time I look up and simply wish I could go there. It works! Slowly, I glide up through the ceiling into complete darkness.

If I've hoped to break through the surface of the water soon, I'm disappointed. I'm pulled to the left by a strong current then flushed through some kind of rectangular water pipe until I spill into a lake that covers half of the floor of a large cave.

Simon stands at the shore, looking at the large stone face behind me. Its mouth is open, as if screaming.

"We've got to go through the mouth," Simon says.

"Isn't that where we just came from?" I ask.

"Maybe. Maybe not. It's entirely possible that this room is just a duplicate of the first one, built to mislead us."

I ask myself who would want to go to all this trouble just to make life more difficult for us, and why. But if I ask Simon, I'll just get one of these answers I don't understand, so I decide not to.

We swim across the lake and step through the mouth. To my relief, there's no staircase inside, but a long, straight passage instead. It opens into a square room seven blocks across, with walls three blocks high, made of gray stone. At the opposite wall is a metal door.

Wooden signs are attached to the upper row of blocks, with writing in a language unknown to me. Below each is a lever, all of them in an upward position. Along the lowest row of blocks are signs almost identical to the ones along the top row, but which read nothing but the word "NO."

"A puzzle room," Simon notes. "We must put the levers into the right positions in order to open that door."

"What's the right position for them?"

"We've got to figure that out according to the signs." He looks at the sign left of the entrance.

"*Mo orsiht niu oye ra,*" I read out loud. "What is that supposed to mean?"

Simon looks at the sign, apparently lost in thought. "Ha!" he exclaims, then he walks on to the next sign. He regards it for a while, then pulls down the lever below it, toward the bottom sign reading "NO."

He pulls down the next lever as well, but leaves the one after that in an upright position. Yes-no-no-yes, that much I understand. But how does he know which lever to pull down? Helplessly, I stare at the foreign messages:

Mo orsiht niu oye ra
Erof ebereh ne ebu oye vah
Eno lauo yera
Dneeht rofg niko olu oy era
Nam red neeht fodi arfa uo yera
Reb meme ru oyod
Rehe volu yod
Htur tehtlle tehsdid
Live wonku oyod
Htur tehte esu oynac

Meanwhile, Simon stands in front of the fifth sign, apparently lost. Finally, he pulls that one down as well, then moves on. He switches down the sixth lever, leaves the seventh and eighth upright, and, after some hesitation, pulls down the final two levers. He looks at the door, which remains closed.

"Hmm," he says, pondering the levers, then goes back to the fifth and pulls it up again.

Nothing happens.

He fumbles with the ninth and tenth levers, but to no avail. I must admit I feel a certain kind of satisfaction watching him getting more and more confused. Apparently, he doesn't really know what he's doing after all.

"Can you read that language?" I ask.

"Sure. Essential adventurer knowledge."

"But still you don't seem to know how to open the door."

"The signs are a bit ... confusing, I must admit."

"I agree. I don't understand a single word."

"Oh, it's easy to read them. But apparently, it's not as easy as I thought to answer the questions on them. I hope we don't have to try out every combination." He makes a brief calculation in his head. "Ten signs, two possible ways of pulling a lever, that makes two to the power of ten combinations, 1,024, to be specific. We probably have to try out more than five hundred combinations before we get that door open by trial and error."

"What are the signs saying?" I ask, impatient.

"Easy. Just read them backwards."

Feeling a bit stupid, I quickly translate the signs:

Are you in this room?
Have you been here before?
Are you alone?
Are you looking for the End?
Are you afraid of the enderman?
Do you remember?
Do you love her?
Did she tell the truth?
Do you know evil?
Can you see the truth?

Now I understand why Simon could pull the first few levers without hesitation: The answers to those questions are pretty obvious. Of course I'm in this room, where else could I be? I sure haven't been here before. I'm not alone. Yes, we're probably looking for the End, according to Simon's explanation. Are we afraid of the enderman? That's where Simon hesitated for the first time. Maybe because there isn't a simple answer to it: Unlike me, he's probably completely unafraid of them.

Do you remember? Simon answered this question with no, probably regarding my amnesia.

The next question is even stranger: *Do you love her?*

Who? Amely? Why is there a question like that on a sign in this room? Simon has left that lever upright. What made him do that? Maybe he figured that I love her from the fact that I asked him about her. But do I really love her? I don't know. I can only remember her sobbing. All I know is that I want to help her.

I pull lever seven down. The door remains closed.

I have no doubt concerning question eight. The doctor in my dream – was it a dream at all? – told me that Amely is schizophrenic. But if someone is lying, it's him.

Question nine: *Do you know evil?* I'm not sure what that means. Simon was unsure as well. But we can just try out both positions.

Last question: *Can you see the truth?* I'm not sure about this lever as well, but Simon has tried out both possibilities. So the problem must lie within the first eight questions.

My companion begins to switch levers, apparently at random, talking to himself all the time. But the door remains closed.

After some time, he stops. "Damn! I don't know which combinations I already tried out!" He sighs. "This is useless. Maybe these levers are just a distraction, and there's a hidden switch somewhere that opens the door. Wouldn't surprise me, after all that happened in this map."

We search every inch, including the corridor that led here, the large cave, even the stone face. We find nothing.

"I'm fed up!" Simon exclaims. He grabs a pickaxe out of nowhere and starts attacking the wall next to the door.

About time we dig our way out of this, I think. But he stops after a few strokes. "I can't believe it! Really!"

"What's wrong?"

"This is no bedrock!" he shouts angrily. "This is just normal stone!"

I wait patiently.

"I can't make a dent in it. I can't even remove the stupid sign!" To prove it, he swings the pickaxe at the wall in a mighty blow. An ugly, cracking sound is heard, and the pickaxe disappears.

"This was my last iron pickaxe!" he says, sounding like he's about to cry any moment. "Apparently, the stupid programmers of this mod have created blocks with completely new properties, making them look like ordinary stone or bedrock."

"Which means what?"

"It means we have to find the correct positions of the levers, or we have to reset the whole map. But, honestly, I'm not sure I'll want to go through all of this again. There's no let's-play clip to be made out of this anyway – nobody's going to believe this crap!"

He makes an exasperated noise. Then he looks at me. "Say, why don't you try attacking the door? You've smashed that bedrock wall, after all!"

I try it. I press against the door, beat at it, kick it, even run into it. To no avail.

"Marco?" someone whispers.

I turn around, startled.

"What is it?" Simon asks. "Did you hear voices again?"

"Yes. Quite close. As if someone else is in this room. Someone we can't see."

"Someone who's here, but isn't," Simon says. "This is getting ever more mysterious."

I'm looking at the levers again. Someone who's here, but isn't. I think about my dream, which may not even have been one.

Are you in this room?

I walk to lever number one and pull it down.

14.

There's bright light. My surroundings are blurred. I'm lying on my back. Something is in my throat that doesn't belong there. I want to pull it out, but I'm unable to move my arms. I can't even turn my head. I feel like I'm trapped in a body that's not mine.

Someone is beside me. I can feel this, but I can't see him or her. I can't even move my eyes to look there.

"Marco?" she whispers.

Amely! I want to shout her name, but my tongue and lips refuse to obey. Not even the faintest whisper escapes my throat.

Darkness creeps up at the edges of my field of vision like evil slime. I'm sinking down into a gloomy shaft. I try to fight it, but there's no way to grab hold of this reality. I shout with all my soul, but there is no sound.

"What's the matter with you?" Simon asks. "Why are you shouting like that? Are you in pain?"

It takes a moment before I can reply. "I'm not here."

"What?"

I ignore his confusion and look at lever number two. Have I been here before?

Yes. I don't know how I know it, but I get a strong feeling of déjà vu. I have been here before. There were different questions on the signs, but apart from that, the room was identical to this one. Only, I wasn't really here. It was ... *as if.*

I'm not sure what that's supposed to mean, but I know it's true. So I pull lever two up.

"Can you tell me what you're doing?" Simon says. He sounds nervous. "What's that supposed to mean, 'you've been here before'? And why aren't you here now? I don't get it!"

"You aren't here either," I say softly. I pull lever three down.

As I turn around, Simon is gone.

"Simon?" I call. "Sir Simon!" I run down the passage, back into the large cave, but he's nowhere to be seen. As if he simply dissolved into thin air. That wasn't what I had in mind.

A deep dejection comes over me. Apparently, I'm lying in a hospital bed, but I can't communicate with those next to me. And now I've lost the only companion I had in this strange Cubeworld. I feel like crying.

After a while, I pull myself together. Maybe I can find my way back to consciousness if I find an exit of the Cubeworld.

I go back to question four: *Are you looking for the End?*

Yes. I need to get out of here!

Are you afraid of the enderman? Definitely.

Do you remember? Do I? My memory is fragmentary at best. I leave the lever at "NO."

Do you love her? Do I love Amely? I'm not sure. I know she's beautiful. It's unlikely that someone like her would ever be interested in me. I confronted her stepfather. Out of love? Probably more out of the feeling that I must help her.

Is that what put me in this mess? Did the doctor do something to me? I can't remember, but the thought is frightening.

I pull down lever seven.

Did she tell the truth? Finally, there's a question I'm quite sure I know the correct answer to: yes.

Do you know evil? I'm not so sure about that. After some

hesitation, I pull the lever up.

Can you see the truth? I look around. This Cubeworld can't be the truth. So I pull that lever down.

The door remains closed.

Damn! I pull the levers I wasn't sure about up and down at random, but to no avail. I'm stuck in the Cubeworld, apparently trapped in my own heavily damaged head.

I look at the levers and think hard. After a while, I realize that I approached the problem in the wrong way. When I pulled the first lever to "NO," I was in reality for a short time. When I switched lever three, Simon vanished.

Maybe this is not about finding the correct combination of levers. Maybe I need to use the levers to change my perception of the Cubeworld. Maybe this very room is the exit I'm looking for all the time, and this door leads right back to reality!

I have already used the first three levers in the right way, I'm sure of that. I'm not quite sure about lever four, but it seems possible that by setting it to the upward position, "YES," it has turned this room into the exit of the Cubeworld.

I stare at lever five *Are you afraid of the enderman?* Those guys with the glowing eyes are creepy. But am I really afraid of them? Yes, I am. Especially now that Simon is gone, I certainly don't want to encounter one of them. Maybe I can simply switch off my fear by pulling the lever down?

I focus on the bad feeling I had when I saw an enderman for the first time. No, I'm not afraid, I tell myself. I pull the lever.

The first thing I feel is a wisp of cold air at my neck. Cold sweat breaks from my pores. I feel it, although in this rectangular body, I neither have pores nor am able to produce sweat.

He's here!

Slowly, I turn around.

I can see him out of the corner of my eye. He looks like the other endermen – large, slim, with long arms like tentacles. But in contrast to his fellows, this one is wearing a white coat.

I feel panic. I shouldn't have pulled that lever down! It was a lie. Now I have to pay for it.

I want to run, but the enderman is blocking the only exit.

Don't look into its eyes, I hear Simon's voice in my head. But its glowing gaze mesmerizes me. My head turns as if someone else moved it with considerable force.

He is here!

He looms over me. His hand grabs my chin, turns my head, so I have to look into his eyes. His face is blurry, but I can see his eyes clearly. They bore into my mind, draining all my willpower away.

"Marco? Can you hear me, Marco?"

I wish I couldn't. I try to close my lids so those eyes will go away, but I can't do even that.

He stares at me. Sweat drenches the sheet I'm lying on.

He smiles. Finally, he pulls back. "Persistent vegetative state," he says. "It is also called 'waking coma.' It has likely been caused by a toxic shock."

"Yes, Dr. Berkholm said the same thing." It's the voice of my mother. She's sitting to the right of me, outside of my field of vision.

"I'm afraid I can't do much about it. But there's a realistic chance that he'll awake on his own."

"Thank you for coming anyway, Doctor."

"Of course. I feel somewhat responsible for his condition. Had I realized sooner how ill he was when he entered my office ... But he appeared so normal ..."

"Please, don't reproach yourself, Doctor. You did all you could. Dr. Berkholm confirmed as much."

"Still, I would like to look after him once in a while, if you don't mind."

"Yes, that would be nice. Please call me immediately if his condition changes."

"Of course." His voice is silky, comforting. A doctor emanating confidence and competence. I bet he's quite popular with his patients.

Don't believe him! I shout. He's the enderman! Don't leave me alone with him!

But nobody can hear me.

I sink down into a dark tunnel to find myself back in the Cubeworld. The enderman stares at me with glowing eyes. He's completely motionless. But as soon as I turn my gaze away, he'll attack. I know I can't withstand him. He'll destroy me.

He already did destroy me!

Where does that thought come from? Is there a scrap of memory? Do I feel a hand at my throat? Is there a soft whisper? *If you move or make a noise, I'll press my thumb into your throat, and you die* ... Do I feel a sting in my side?

With the realization, there comes rage. "You did it!" I shout. "While I talked to you, you secretly prepared a syringe. In my rage, I wasn't watching what you were doing. You laughed at me, called my accusations 'figments.' Then, all of a sudden you were behind me. You grabbed my throat and injected something into me. I felt weak and dropped onto the floor. The last thing I heard was you shouting for help."

The enderman regards me without moving. His silence is like a confession.

"You bloody bastard!" Like a berserker, I slash at him with my sword.

The enderman doesn't defend himself. He just stands there, staring at me with his glowing eyes, which somehow have lost their power over me. I'm not afraid of him anymore. I can see his eyes widen. Now he's the one who's afraid! I know that the truth is stronger than all his power, and he knows it as well.

A last blow, and my foe vanishes with a plop. He leaves an ender pearl behind, which I pick up.

Lever five is now in the correct position: No, I'm not afraid of the enderman anymore. And yes, I remember what happened before I fell into a coma. I pull lever six up.

The door remains shut.

Do you love her?

Will that lever also have some effect on my memory? I pull it up as well.

I'm in the schoolyard. She's standing by the side, alone. Her shoulders slumped, her long dark curls half covering her face. She wears blue jeans, a sweater, and a gray jacket, nothing fancy.

I have often seen her like this. She's attended our school for half a year, but she doesn't seem to have any friends. Maybe I should talk to her. I have thought about that many times before, searching for words that wouldn't sound embarrassing. So far, I haven't been able to think of any.

Bam! A ball hits me hard at the shoulder, accompanied by loud laughter.

I turn around.

"Love makes the world go round, doesn't it, dude?" cries Victor Bourne, who threw the ball. The others, who have stopped playing soccer in order to watch me, hoot and laugh at this. Victor is the clown in our class. Most of the time, his quips are kind of funny, but he usually makes them at the expense of someone else. In this case, I'm the prey.

I can't make the mistake of defending myself now, or, even worse, getting mad at him. So I put on a flirtatious look. "Oh, Vicky, finally you realize what I'm feeling for you!" I purr.

It's a bit stupid, I admit, but it works. The others roar with laughter. Victor is at a loss for the moment. He's not used to being the subject of jokes. But he knows the rules of the schoolyard as well as I do. "Are you going to take me for a cup of coffee later, sweetie?" he asks.

"Sure, honey pie!"

With that, our little exchange is over. Victor wanders off in search of easier prey.

I turn to see that Amely has lifted her head. She's looking at me. Did she overhear that the boys were making fun of me, because of her?

Her eyes shine. She looks down at the ground again.

I don't think. My legs are a bit wobbly as I walk over to her, and there's a lump in my throat. I have no idea what to say. All I can think of is "Hi!"

She doesn't answer, just continues staring at her feet.

"Are you ... okay?" I ask.

She looks up. Her eyes are red. Either she's ill, or she's about to cry. "Please leave me alone," she says. "I'm fine."

She's not a very talented liar.

I linger for a moment, while she looks down again. After

a minute or so, I move away.

"Do I have to be jealous now?" Victor asks as we go back to class. I just ignore him.

In the following weeks, I approach Amely again and again. Sometimes I talk to her; sometimes I just stand beside her in silence. I'm the scorn of the class, but the whispering behind my back hardly registers with me.

No, whatever the others think, I'm not in love with her. At least I don't think I am - I'm not really sure about my own feelings. In any case, love is not the reason for my approaching her.

I can feel she needs me. I think I knew that from the first moment I saw her. Our brief eye contact was like a cry for help. She wants to tell me something, but she can't. She mustn't.

I think about talking to our homeroom teacher, asking her for help. I get along quite well with her. But Amely might see that as a breach of our trust, although she hasn't told me anything yet.

So I just wait.

On a bright October day I stand beside her in the schoolyard, about five feet apart, when I hear her voice, little more than a whisper: "You mustn't tell anyone!"

I turn around. She stares at the ground.

I take a step toward her. "Promise."

"He gives me pills. If he ever finds out I'm not taking them ..."

"Who?"

"My ... my stepfather."

The bell rings for the end of recess. But this is more important than English class. "Come," I say.

Without turning around, I walk through the large

wrought-iron gate. It is strictly forbidden to leave the schoolyard during school hours, but we can't simply stay in plain sight of everyone.

She follows.

For a while, we walk through the neighborhood in silence.

"What kind of pills?" I ask.

"Tranquilizers," she says. "They make you numb, like your body is made of rubber. You don't care about anything."

"Why does he make you take them?"

"So I keep quiet. So I don't … struggle."

I stop in my tracks, staring at her. "So you don't struggle?"

She doesn't answer. Her lower lip trembles. Tears stream down her cheeks.

I put my arms around her. She cries against my shoulder.

"You … you must talk to the police!" I say.

It takes a moment for her to answer. "They won't believe me. He's a doctor. For years now, he has claimed that I'm schizophrenic and have hallucinations. They'd just put me into a mental hospital."

"What about your mother?"

She doesn't answer. I just wait until she's ready.

After a long time, she pulls back from me. Her tears have dried. "He controls her." Her voice is flat, like she's reading something boring from a book.

She tells me about the hell she has lived in for years now. Her parents split up when she was six. Her mother fell into a deep depression then went to a doctor, who prescribed her medication. He started making visits to her

94

home with increasing frequency. Finally, even Amely understood that his therapy for her mother consisted of more than pills. He was always nice to her, like a doctor is nice to kids. She never liked him very much, but her mother seemed to feel better after his visits.

Then one day, she realized that her mother's good mood was just a result of the strong medication he gave her. When the effect wore off, her depression just got worse. Nevertheless, the doctor came almost daily, until he finally moved in with them.

When Amely was nine, he declared that she had to take pills, too. She didn't want to, but he forced her. Then, when she was in this strange state, when nothing hurt and she didn't care at all, when her mother was sleeping a drugged sleep, he came to her room and did things to her.

She doesn't tell me what kind of things. She doesn't have to.

"Please, you must never tell anybody, ever!" she pleads. "Otherwise ... he's going to kill me!"

"But ... but we must do something! We can't just ..."

"Promise it! Please!"

"Okay, I promise."

"Thank you!" She cries at my shoulder again. "Thank you for listening!"

I pull her closer to me, softly stroking her back. Her sobs increase in intensity, but I sense it's relief that makes her cry even harder.

Do you love her?

Yes. I think I fell in love with her at that moment: when she trusted me with her secret for the first time. After she told me about her torments, I didn't just feel sorry for her anymore. We were now sharing a terrible secret. We were in it together. I would die to protect her, if need be. And I know she'd do the same for me. If that isn't love, what is?

Did she tell the truth?

Now I understand the true meaning of the question: It's not about the description of her agony or the statement that her father is the evildoer. It's about her answer to the first question I asked her: "Are you okay?"

"Please leave me alone. I'm fine," was what she said.

I pull lever eight down to "NO."

Do you know evil?

I think of Amely's tale. I hear the scornful laughter as I confront her stepfather with the accusations. I feel his hand at my throat.

A doctor who's exploiting the trust of his patients, making them docile with medication, only to abuse them: There can't be anything more evil. Lever nine stays at "YES."

Can you see the truth?

I stare at the sign for a while. By now, I know that I'm lying in a hospital. But is that the answer to the question?

What do I see? A room made of stone blocks, a lot of signs and levers, a closed door. That is not the truth.

I pull the lever up.

The room disappears.

15.

My mother bends over me. Her face appears fuzzy, but I recognize the smell of her perfume. In spite of my predicament, it kindles a cozy feeling of comfort.

"Marco! Oh, my poor boy!" she whispers. A tear drops onto my cheek. My skin twitches slightly.

Her eyes widen. "Marco? Marco, can you hear me?"

I want to reply, but my throat is still paralyzed. I try to create any kind of reaction, moving my head or at least a finger. But the connection between my brain and my muscles seems to be severed. I'm trapped in a body that doesn't obey me anymore.

Gathering all my willpower, I manage to blink.

"Marco!" My mother's voice sounds startled. "Marco, if you can hear me, please blink twice!"

I close my eyes briefly once, then again.

She sobs. She kisses me and hugs me. "Doctor!" she shouts. "Doctor Berkholm! Come quickly!" She runs out of the room.

I'm not sure whether I should be happy about this. What if I stay like this forever, only being able to communicate by blinking? What a horrendous thought! I'd rather stay in that strange world where I'm wandering around in my dream state.

The Cubeworld. Now I remember being in it often, long before I got into this mess. I have explored caves, beat monsters, built castles. I survived adventures and solved riddles and quests. I stood in a room full of levers and found the combination that opened the metal door at the other end. Endermen and creepers didn't frighten me. It was just a game, after all.

It's called Minecraft.

I remember watching tons of let's-play videos on YouTube. In some of them, a guy named Simon played the game. He was kind of funny, always doing the wrong thing, creating hilarious situations. One day, my mother looked over my shoulder, shaking her head in disbelief. She didn't get why I preferred these clips over the TV cartoon shows. "What's so interesting about watching someone else playing a computer game?" she asked. I didn't even try to explain. She wouldn't have understood anyway.

The Cubeworld became kind of a second home to me. Countless hours were spent there. I met new friends on various Minecraft servers. I began creating my own adventure maps as a challenge for other players. Even though the cube graphics seemed a bit outdated compared to the sleek games on my Xbox, I loved this game more than any other. Instead of just walking around, solving the quests others had put there, I could change the environment and even create my own world. This endless creative freedom was what totally grabbed me.

No wonder my dream world was created after this model.

Was it some kind of self-protection of my brain that led to me being trapped in this dream? Or has the stuff Amely's stepfather injected into me destroyed parts of my brain? It appears like the damage is not permanent, for piece by piece, I have gotten my memory back.

I now remember being in a small hut with three signs. One read: "The exit lies in the Nether. Save Amely. M." Was that a message of my subconscious? Is the path through the Cubeworld like some kind of system reset of my nervous system?

Have I already reached my goal?

No, I haven't, I realize. Far from it. I now remember a lot, but I still can't move. Blinking may be the way to communicate to my mother to show I can hear her. But how can I tell her what happened? How can I warn her against that "nice" doctor who cares about my well-being in such a "touching" way?

The realization hits me like the blow of an enderman's arm: If he becomes aware of my waking from my coma, he's going to kill me! As soon as he's alone with me, he'll press a pillow over my face or inject an overdose of the stuff he used to send me to sleep. It will look like I just didn't make it. Nobody will get suspicious of him.

Even worse: Amely will pay the price for my boldness.

I must put a stop to that bastard's evil deeds! I must wake up! In order to do that, I must continue down the path that my subconscious has prepared for me, and quickly.

I search for a picture of the room with the levers inside my mind. I focus on it, falling down a deep, black well. At the edge of my consciousness, I realize that my mother is coming back with the doctor.

She'll wait in vain for a reaction from me. I'm sorry to disappoint her, but there is no alternative.

I'm standing in the lever room again. The stupid metal door is still closed, although I am sure now that all levers are in their correct position.

I regard them again:

Are you in this room? No.
Have you been here before? Yes.
Are you alone? Yes.
Are you looking for the End? Yes.

Are you afraid of the enderman? No.
Do you remember? Yes.
Do you love her? Yes.
Did she tell the truth? No.
Do you know evil? Yes.
Can you see the truth? Yes.

What the heck is wrong? I think about systematically testing each lever a second time, but refrain from it. The levers had a direct effect on my perception of this world. I might be doing damage if I put a lever in the wrong position. For example, what if I pull lever five to yes, and then panic at the sight of an enderman? That might make it impossible for me to finish my journey. Or what if I push lever six down and lose all the memories I have gathered so painstakingly?

Just randomly trying levers is too dangerous. I have to solve this riddle by thinking.

Maybe my memories of countless hours playing Minecraft might help.

I now understand why Simon was so upset when we encountered things that, according to the Minecraft rules, are impossible.

I remember a sentence he said when we beat the endermen and opened the treasure chest: "Blaze powder. I don't like this at all!"

At the time, I had no idea what blaze powder was, so I wondered about his reaction. Now I understand.

I've been to the End only once before. It's a dark, eerie place, where there's no turning back. I fought the Enderdragon but stood no chance against it. Whenever I struck it with my sword, it was healed by beams from magic crystals placed on large pillars. At some point, I simply gave up and died. I remember thinking that killing the Enderdragon was simply impossible. Not even Notch, the creator of Minecraft, could beat that monster.

Just then I realize that I don't want to go to the End – especially in this dream world that is so frighteningly real. What if the Enderdragon kills me in this state? Will I be dead in reality as well? That seems all too likely.

I remember another thing: "The exit lies in the Nether," said the sign in the hut. Not "The exit lies in the End."

Relief floods through me. The Nether is bad enough, if I think about all the monsters I already met down there. But at least, there is no Enderdragon.

No, I am not looking for the End. I am looking for the exit!

I pull lever four down.

There is a soft click. As I turn, I can see the metal door open wide.

Beyond it is a short corridor, lit by torches. At the end, there's a staircase winding upward in a rectangular spiral.

I climb hundreds of steps. In reality, I'd long be out of breath, but here I don't feel any exertion at all.

From somewhere upstairs, I can hear the telltale sounds of zombies and skeletons. I draw my sword.

The staircase ends in a small room with a wooden door at one end. Behind it, there's an irregular cave, and a large mass of monsters waiting for me.

I open the door, stepping aside so the arrows shot by skeletons can't hit me.

Immediately, the first zombies storm inside, and the battle begins.

I bash up a few dozen of the sinister fiends until my

health gets dangerously close to zero. With some effort, I manage to close the door.

The cave is still filled to the brim with monsters. There are probably a few spawners out there, generating limitless numbers of monsters.

What am I supposed to do now? I'm healing, but I also feel my empty stomach, and I have no food with me. When I'm hungry, my wounds won't heal anymore. Sooner or later, the hunger itself will also drain my life energy.

If only I had some wood, I could create a workbench, make a pickaxe, and just dig around the cave. But stupid as I was, I gave Simon all his items back when he awoke. All I have are the sword and armor.

Once again, I'm in deep trouble.

I peer through the small windows set in the door. On the other side, there's a creeper, staring at me with his strangely sad face.

"Get lost!" I shout, irritated. "Leave me alone!"

The creeper moves a step back, as if shocked. Then he comes closer again.

Am I just imagining this, or did he really react to my shouting?

"I said, 'Get lost!'" I bellow as loudly as possible.

Again, the creeper moves back. But the effect doesn't last long. As soon as I stop shouting, the monster closes in again.

Can I vanquish the monsters just by yelling at them? Of course, in the real Minecraft game, that wouldn't work. But this reality I created myself.

I get an idea. "Creative mode!" I shout. But there's no endless supply of materials in my head, like there would be in the game if I entered creative mode.

Obviously, it's not that easy.

Maybe I need to listen to my subconscious a little more. I should try to interpret the messages it sends me, if I ever hope to get out of here.

Then I realize what it is trying to tell me: What could get me out of this mess, what might give me back some control over myself, is anger.

It isn't really hard to get angry. Not at all. All I have to do is think of Amely's tears when she told me about her ordeal, and of her stepfather laughing as I confronted him with his deeds.

I pull open the door. "You stupid assholes!" I roar.

Dozens of skeletons, zombies, and creepers stare at me, apparently flabbergasted. Some of them take a step back.

"You freakin' idiots think you can mess with me, yeah? Get away, if your meager existence has any worth to you! Or I'll turn you into zombie stew with bone meal!"

The monsters draw back even farther. A creeper at the edge of the crowd even explodes out of shock, drawing a few monsters with it to oblivion.

It works! If I continue to shout at them, I can get to the small exit at the far end of the cave without being attacked.

Unfortunately, I never was the type who swore a lot. My supply of swearwords is quite limited. I simply can't think of anything else to shout at them.

The monsters make monster noises and draw nearer. Already, an arrow flies. Damn!

In my desperation, a memory from my childhood flashes in my mind. *The Adventures of Tintin* was my favorite comic book series. And the character I loved most was Captain Haddock, who swore all the time.

"Billions of bilious blue blistering barnacles!" I roar.

"Ten thousand thundering typhoons!"

The monsters flee in panic, tumbling over one another as they try to get away from me.

"Pirates! Troglodytes! Kleptomaniacs! Sea gherkins! Freshwater swabs!"

I run to the exit as fast as I can, searching my memory for more swearwords.

"Gobbledygooks! Filibusters! Pockmarks! Guano gatherers! Baboons! Hydrocarbons! Two-timing Tartar twisters! Balkan beetles! Hooligans! Pickled herrings! Crab apples! Mamelukes! Prattling porpoises!"

I burst into laughter. I really can't help it. This is too ridiculous!

The monsters seem to be angered by my laughter. They storm toward me from all sides.

I run as fast as I can. Just as I reach the exit, an arrow hits me in the back, and for a moment, I get dizzy. I turn around. "Are you crazy?" I shout. "That hurt!"

The skeleton pursuing me stops in its tracks. It looks at me as if it is sorry.

"Leave me alone, dammit!" I shout, turning around and walking away without giving the monsters a further glance.

After a while, the *unngh*s and clicking noises quiet down. Total darkness surrounds me. I stumble forward, running into walls and corners, but somehow I manage to follow the irregular path. I can only hope that there's no hole somewhere in front of me.

Is there a faint glow farther down the path?

It's no mirage. After a few bends, the tunnel widens and I see daylight shining brightly. I'm back at the surface!

But the view that awaits me when I step out of the cave entrance is completely unexpected.

16

I am standing on top of a steep mountainside. Below me, there's a wide valley with a river meandering through it. It is bordered by buildings of all kinds – small huts and impressive palaces, towers higher than a mountain as well as featureless gray cubes without doors or windows. Strange structures are scattered throughout, shaped like objects: One looks like a giant mushroom, another reminds me of a boot, a third is a giant tree, its trunk riddled with windows and balconies. All in all, it looks like a crazy architect has built all his most absurd creations in one place.

Some of these constructions appear strangely familiar. Then I remember that I have built them myself while learning to play Minecraft.

What is my subconscious trying to tell me with this? Is there a message behind all of these structures?

In any case, I need something to eat and I need equipment. If I want to get to the Nether, I must create an obsidian portal. It's possible to make one using a very hard material formed by cooling lava with water. Not a big deal, if you know how to do it.

I climb down the mountainside and approach the city. As I come closer, I can see that the outer buildings are built side by side, leaving no space in between, with no doors where I am. So I have to walk for a while until I find a passage. It is guarded by a guy with a light blue shirt and dark blue trousers.

"Hi!" I say.

My mirror image doesn't answer. He seems to look at me with distrust, although I can't really read his unmoving expression. In any case, he's standing in my way.

"Please, let me pass!" I ask.

He doesn't react.

I try to move beside him, but the passage is too narrow. I could try to find another entrance into the city, but I have a hunch that I would run into the same problem. Obviously, this is another trial laid out for me by my subconscious.

I cast some serious Haddockish curses at him, without making an impression. At least, he dignifies me with an answer: "Strangers are not allowed to enter!"

His voice sounds odd. It takes me a moment to realize why: It is my own voice, sounding like it does on a voice box - sounding like others hear it.

"I'm not a stranger!" I say.

"You're not in the city, therefore you are a stranger!"

Great logic! If everyone who's not in the city is a stranger and can't enter, how did anybody get *in* in the first place?

I wonder whether my mirror image doesn't recognize me because of my armor. I take it off. "See, I look just like you!" I explain. "In fact, I *am* you! I'm not a stranger!"

He regards me for a moment. "You are not me. I am me."

"You are a part of me. A projection of my subconscious, to be specific. So let me pass!"

"Strangers are not allowed to enter!"

I didn't know that buried somewhere deep within me, there's a stubborn clerk's mind.

The sky is turning orange. If I stand here much longer, I'll have to deal with monsters.

I improvise. "But I have to get into the city. I've got an urgent message for the king!"

"You've got a message for the king?" he asks suspiciously.

"Yes!" I assure him. "If you don't let me pass this instant, he's going to put you in chains and lock you up in his dungeon!"

"He's going to put me in chains?"

"Yes, he will! Now let me pass!"

"Strangers are not allowed to enter!"

I'm fed up. Now I can understand when my parents always claimed it was difficult to make me change my mind. I put on my armor and draw my sword.

"I don't want to use force, but ..."

The guard stares at the sword. "Alarm!" he shouts at the top of his rectangular lungs. "Alarm!" He runs off.

Oh boy, now I'm a hostile intruder in my own subconscious! I briefly wonder what a psychiatrist would make of it.

I'm prepared to face an army of heavily armored knights the next instant. If I'm lucky, they'll catch me and throw me in some dungeon. If I'm unlucky, I'll die. Maybe then I'll awake in Simon's hut, without remembering anything that happened in the meantime.

But there's no army approaching. The guard is nowhere to be seen. Maybe he fled into one of the houses. The street before me lies empty. Actually, the whole city looks empty and lifeless.

Maybe the guy I just scared away was the only inhabitant! What does that say about my condition? Nothing good, I'm afraid.

I push the problem away and focus on my immediate concerns. First, I need food. I open the door to a house that looks relatively normal in this strange neighborhood. It is built of stone blocks, with two stories and a peaked wooden roof.

Inside, it is lit with torches, which cast a cozy light. A stone oven has a reddish glow. Beside it, there's a workbench and a large chest. A ladder on one wall leads up through an opening in the ceiling.

I look into the oven and discover a piece of grilled meat. I devour it on the spot, satisfying my hunger for the time being. Next, I open the chest.

It contains everything useful in this world: pickaxes, axes, and swords made of diamond, an armor of the same material, lots of bread, wooden cubes and iron bars, potions of healing, and many other valuable items. I pick up as much as my mind can hold.

Just as I'm about to leave the house, I hear a voice from above: "Marco? Is that you?"

A shiver runs down my spine. It's my mother's voice.

I climb - no, I glide up the ladder. Upstairs, there's a comfortable room with slanting walls. Two beds are standing side by side. A fireplace on one wall is lit. Beside it stands a woman, who is staring at me.

She has a boxlike bosom and wears a pink dress. She doesn't look like my mother at all, but the voice is unmistakable.

"Finally you've come home, Marco!" she says.

"This is not my home," I state.

"How can you say that, my son?" She sounds disappointed. "Come, let me embrace you!"

She approaches me, extending her box arms and wrapping them around me. It feels strangely good. Despite her rectangular forms, I sense her soft, motherly body. I even recognize her perfume. The urge to sink into these arms, get lost in them, completely entrust myself to them, is overwhelming. But something keeps me alert.

I pull myself away from her. "Who are you?"

"What is that question supposed to mean? I'm your mother, Marco!"

"I doubt that. You're just part of my imagination!"

"Nonsense. You're playing too many computer games!"

"We *are* in a computer game! Or at least, in a dream of a computer game."

She simply ignores my objection, like she often does. "Now sit down and eat something, then you can rest. It was a long day." She holds out a bowl filled with brown mash that smells lovely, like spaghetti carbonara. It's her special recipe, with lots of cream, fresh eggs, mild bacon, and a pinch of nutmeg.

I'm not hungry anymore, but I still take the bowl and eat. It tastes like heaven. Suddenly I feel such a longing to be home again that I break into tears.

"But you are home!" my virtual mother says, as if she has read my mind. "Now lie down and rest!" She points to one of the beds.

I'm not really tired, but the thought of lying down for a while is enticing. It would also have the advantage that I'll wake up in this house next time I die, instead of in Simon's hut.

Still, I hesitate. I feel a vague uneasiness. Something isn't quite right.

"What's wrong?" "Mom" asks. "Don't you like it here?"

"I'm sorry, but I must move on."

"Now? In the middle of the night? That's much too dangerous! Think of the enderman!"

The way she says it, with a threatening tone, raises my

suspicions. "I'll deal with him," I say. "I've got diamond armor and lots of potions of healing!"

She laughs brightly. "Don't be ridiculous, my son! Nobody can overcome the enderman!"

"I vanquished him once before. I can do it again."

"Yes, my son, tomorrow perhaps," she says softly. "But first, you need to sleep!" She extends her arm and touches my shoulder. A deep tiredness begins to overtake me.

"I ... I need to ..." I'm not sure anymore what I intended to say.

"Lie down and close your eyes, my treasure. All will be well!"

I concentrate on the image of Amely's face. "I can't. I need to carry on. Now!"

"That is quite out of the question!" she says with the voice she always uses when she won't tolerate any further discussion. "You're going to sleep first!"

"No!" I take a step toward the ladder.

Quickly, she blocks my way. "You can't go out there now! Think of the monsters!"

"I don't care about the monsters! Get out of my way!"

"You're much too young to stay awake this long! You're going to bed right now!" I can feel that she's about to get really mad.

"You can't tell me what to do!"

"But I'm your mother!"

"No, you're not! My mother is waiting for me in reality. That's where I'm going right now! Let me pass!"

"Go ... to ... bed ... now!" she hisses. Her face gets green, and her body begins to swell, as if she's about to burst out of anger. She's looking almost like ... a creeper!

I barely manage to take two steps backwards before my

mother explodes. A heavy shock hits me, but it doesn't kill me. Where she stood, there's a gaping hole in the floor. A part of the wall and roof are gone. I can see stars shining, and hear *unngh*s and clicking noises.

I drink a potion of healing, jump down through the hole, and leave the house.

While the street was deserted during dusk, it is now full of life. No, that's the wrong term. The inhabitants wandering around between the strange houses aren't really alive. Dozens of zombies and skeletons are strolling through the night. They wear clothes in many different colors. Some even wear rectangular hats. There are tiny zombies and tiny skeletons running around between them like undead kids.

A door opens and a skeleton steps out onto the street. I don't like the fact that these monsters can walk through doors.

On the other hand, so far the undead remain unaggressive. They walk past me and don't even seem to take notice of me. Maybe they can't see me for some reason. Once in a while, they exchange *unngh*s and clicks, as if chatting.

Keeping my eyes down, I follow the street toward the city center. I try to make sense of what I just experienced, without much success. Meeting my false mother was quite disturbing. It proved that I can't trust my own subconscious.

I consider simply digging my way into the ground, finding some lava, turning it into obsidian by cooling it with water, and creating a Nether portal. After all, I have all the equipment I need. But something drives me forward instead. This strange city must have some kind of purpose.

Maybe it's a good idea to find out what it is before I enter the Nether.

The guard didn't object when I was talking of a message for the king, so maybe there is, in fact, a king or ruler in this city. Maybe I should talk to him.

Or maybe it's the stupidest idea I ever had. There's only one way to find out.

I remember seeing a large palace near the center of the city. I'm not sure in which direction to go, though. I briefly consider asking a zombie for the way. Then decide maybe not.

After wandering around for a while, I come across a large marketplace with lots of stands. Zombies and skeletons sell glowing pumpkins, rotten flesh, and rectangular body parts to other zombies and skeletons.

The bustle unexpectedly turns into a lot more commotion. Searching for the source, I realize that the light is gradually changing. Dawn breaks.

The sellers hastily pack their wares while the crowd leaves the marketplace. As the sun rises, the last of the undead scurry away. A zombie can't reach the entrance of his house in time and bursts into flame. He's making desperate *unngh* noises, blindly staggering across the street. Nobody's there to help him. I almost feel sorry for him. After a minute or so, he simply dissolves into smoke, leaving a piece of rotten flesh behind.

I walk along deserted streets. I reach a giant tower, at least a hundred blocks high. I'd sure have an excellent view from up there. But I cringe at the thought of entering the tower, the home for probably hundreds of undead. Maybe they wouldn't remain neutral toward me if I entered their bedrooms. So I move on.

Around noon, I reach another large, open square. On one side of it is the giant palace I was looking for. Broad steps lead toward a portal of columns. Behind it, a large rectangular building rises, with a turret on each corner.

I know the architecture of this place well. I have designed it, after all. It is one of the largest buildings I ever created in Minecraft. It may not be very elegant, but it is certainly impressive. If there is a king of the undead in this city, this is where he will be found. And it's not hard to figure out what kind of king that would be, for in the middle of the plaza, there's a statue of an enderman, at least twenty blocks high.

I climb up the steps and walk through the portal. Behind it, a short alley leads to the palace gate. It is locked, and there seems to be no way to open it. In my original design, there was a button beside the gate. It is missing now.

I could try to make a hole in the wall, but that would certainly alert some guards. So I better wait until the sun sets again.

In the meantime, I explore the surrounding streets. One of the houses in the vicinity looks like an upside-down pyramid, another resembles a ship that run aground, but mostly the buildings look quite normal. It's a strange feeling walking through this alien city, knowing it was I who created it. In a way, I should be a god in this world. But I seem to have no superhuman powers now, and feel more like a prisoner.

The sun finally sets. In short order, the streets fill with undead. As before, they ignore me, running their incomprehensible errands.

I briefly wonder what will happen when I reach my goal and wake up. Will this world simply cease to exist? It is a slightly depressing thought.

As I reach the palace gate, it stands wide open, but a zombie and a skeleton guard it, both equipped with iron armor and swords.

"*Unngh?*" the zombie asks.

"I need to see the king," I say.

"*Unngh!*" he replies. Both of them stay where they are.

I sigh, drawing my sword. If there's no way to avoid it ... But suddenly I have an idea.

"*Unngh, unngh unngh, unngh!*" I exclaim. I don't have the slightest idea if this zombielike stammering has any meaning to them at all. Maybe I just uttered undeadly insults.

But the zombie guard just nods his head, says "*Unngh,*" and steps aside.

Flabbergasted, I stand for a moment. Finally, I step through the gate before he can change his mind.

I walk down a corridor with red carpet that leads to a large room with high windows. The floor is covered with a chessboard pattern of stone and obsidian. Giant pillars hold up a ceiling ten blocks high. Large paintings on the walls depict sinister scenes from the world of the undead.

The only source of light comes from two large fireplaces, one on the left wall and one on the right wall. At the far end of the room stands a large throne on top of a pedestal, apparently made of something like ivory. An enderman sits on it. The path to the throne is lined with zombies and skeletons who stare at me in silence.

"Welcome, Marco!"

The voice of the enderman is like the rustling of old paper. He speaks softly, but I understand every word as if he whispered it directly into my ear. A shiver runs down my spine. I get the feeling that it was a bad idea to come here. But it's too late to turn around now.

"Come to me!" the enderman commands.

My legs move on their own, as if he controls them. I keep my eyes down. My heart beats quickly. I can hear it, like the beating of a large drum somewhere deep in this grim palace. Is it the heart of my cube body, or the real one?

I reach the steps that lead up to the pedestal.

"Look at me!" the king of the undead commands.

I want to resist, but it's like an invisible hand grabs my chin, pulling it upward.

The eyes of the enderman glow, but there seems to be no evil in them. Instead they look gentle, even benevolent.

"You don't need to be afraid of me," he says with his expressionless voice.

"Who ... who are you?" I ask.

"You know who I am," he answers. "After all, you came here looking for me."

I want to object - I need to tell him that I'm here only out of curiosity, that I have no idea what he's talking about. But I can't make a sound. For he is right: I know perfectly well who he is.

He is the enderman - he who ends all.

Before me, on his pale throne, sits Death himself.

17

I want to run away, but I just stand, transfixed. The black figure's gaze traps me.

"It's good that you came," Death whispers. "Everything ends here."

"No!" I protest. "I don't want to die!"

"Don't fight it. It won't hurt."

I draw my sword. "Never! I've defeated you before. More than once. I'll not retreat now!" But the resolve I try to put in my voice sounds fragile.

"You cannot defeat me," Death says. "Nobody can. You can run away for a while, deny my existence, but in the end you'll stand before me again like anyone else."

"We'll see about that!" I shout. I wave my diamond sword around, but I can feel my strength dwindle at the same time, without the enderman even touching me.

"You humans are afraid of me," he rasps. "But there is no reason. There's nothing bad about not existing. You didn't exist for billions of years before you were born. How did that feel? Was it in any way unpleasant? There's no difference between that and the state you'll be in after you submit yourself to me. I'm gentle to everyone who's willing to accept my embrace. I only hurt you if you decide to fight me."

I want to protest and shout at him, but I don't have the power. The sword in my hand feels heavy. As if from a far distance, I hear an alarm beeping. Frantic steps, a shout: "Dr. Berkholm!"

"Please!" I plead. "I mustn't die! I have to help Amely stop her stepfather! Please let me wake up, just once, so I can tell her the truth! Then you can have me!"

Death scrutinizes me for a while. "You're willing to give yourself to me, just to help Amely?"

The whole room sways. I can hardly keep upright. Something constricts my throat. "Yes, I am!" I croak.

"All right, I grant you a reprieve." Death raises his arm. It feels as if a heavy weight is lifted from my breast. At last, I can breathe freely. "But I can't make you wake up. You must find the path to yourself on your own."

I take a few deep breaths. The air in my lungs feels wonderful. "I need to get to the Nether," I say. "The exit lies down there. I think."

"In the Nether? I doubt it," says Death. "There's no exit down there to any other world than this one. The only exit to the outside leads through the End. But it's a very dangerous one."

I'm confused. The sign read "The exit lies in the Nether," but Simon thought we had to go through the End. Is Death right?

"Do you see the doors to the left and right?" Death points in both directions with his arms. "Behind one door lies a portal to the Nether, and behind the other lies a portal to the End. Decide which way you want to go. But decide carefully, because there is no way back! I wish you luck and I'm already looking forward to our next meeting!" Death seems to grin, although he doesn't have any recognizable mouth.

I open the door to the left. In the middle of the room behind it, there's a black square in the floor, three blocks long by three blocks wide. It is flanked by four rows of green blocks with round eyes in them. These are ender eyes, which are crafted from ender pearls and blaze powder. Above the black square, purple sparks dance in the air, indicating that the portal is activated.

Small gray beings scurry around – silverfish. Not very strong, they can get quite nasty if they appear in swarms. But the animals show no aggressiveness toward me. In the palace of Death, things are strangely peaceful.

I regard the portal. Just one step, and I'm in the End. There I'll meet the dreadful Enderdragon. The thought alone makes me sick.

No, I'm not ready yet to stand up to that challenge.

I close the door and enter the opposite room. In contrast to the End portal, the Nether portal stands upright. It measures five blocks by four blocks, and has a frame of obsidian. In the middle, a purple energy field wavers. A strange machinelike humming and hissing emanates from it.

I already built a couple of Nether portals, so I know that unlike End portals, there's another portal at the far side, which always makes it possible to return. Therefore, I can explore the Nether and, if I don't find the exit down there, I can always come back and try the End later.

This thought decides it. I take a deep breath and step through the portal.

I get a dizzy feeling, like riding a roller coaster. I briefly black out. The next moment I find myself in a giant cave made of dark red stone. Here and there, clusters of yellowish glowstone hang from the ceiling. A stream of lava flows down into a large lava lake.

It is strangely silent. Only the occasional blubbering of the lava fills the cave. The humming and hissing form of the Nether portal is gone.

I turn around. Behind me, there's nothing but reddish netherrack. There's no way back to the palace of Death.

Once again, I'm trapped!

I realize that I acted hastily. Didn't Death warn me that I should choose my path carefully? Didn't he make it clear that there would be no way back? Unwittingly, I took that to mean "from the End," assuming that the Nether portal would work both ways, as usual. I didn't take into account that my subconscious doesn't care much about the game's rules.

Now I'm trapped down here, with no way back to the Overworld. I don't have any obsidian blocks I could use to create another portal, and in the Nether, there's no water to cool down lava. My only chance is to find the exit to reality, if it exists down here.

I could simply jump into the lava lake. If you die in the Nether, you normally wake up just where you slept last time in the Overworld. At least, that's the case in the real game. But here? Would Death give me another chance? I doubt it.

To make bad things worse, I hear a wailing sound, as if from a baby. Somewhere in the vicinity, there's a ghast!

These large, jellyfish-like creatures float through the air and shoot fireballs at unwitting adventurers. They aren't the worst kind of enemy you find in the Nether, but they're bad enough.

It doesn't take long until a ghast floats around a corner, coming directly toward me. Its rectangular tentacles move back and forth, as if it is galloping along an invisible bridge. As it sees me, it casts a wailing howl and shoots a fireball at me.

I know what to do. But it's one thing to do it in front of a computer screen, moving a mouse, and quite another to stand in this cave, in a world that feels absolutely real, while a large fireball roars toward me. I raise my sword in order to deflect the missile, but I lash out too early.

The fireball hits the ground next to me and explodes. Thrown aside, I suffer a lot of damage, while some of the netherrack blocks burst into flame.

I jump away hastily, while another fireball explodes behind me. The ghast wails, as if offended that I didn't hold still in order to let it roast me.

I manage to gulp down a potion of healing and raise my sword just in time for the next fireball. This time, my timing is better. I hit the glowing hot ball at the right instant. The effect is about the same as hitting an armed hand grenade with a tennis racket. The fireball flies right back to its creator, where it explodes with a loud bang.

I hop around like Andre Agassi at his best. Another fireball approaches. I return it over the invisible net with an elegant forehand volley. With an eerie babylike cry, the ghast dies. Its remains tumble into the lava lake. Game, set, and match, Marco!

The joy over my victory doesn't last very long. If I can't find a way out of the Nether, I'll perish sooner or later. And I have enough reason to believe that my survival in the Cubeworld is closely tied to the fate of my real body in the hospital bed.

This is no game anymore.

I wander along the shore of the lake. At one end, the cave narrows down to a tunnel a few blocks high, only to open up into another cave shortly thereafter. This one is even bigger than the one I came from. Three lava falls gush from the ceiling down into another large lake. At the far end, I recognize rectangular black features: a Nether fortréss. The sight raises my hopes. Nether fortresses are unpleasant places full of nasty surprises, but if there's an exit somewhere here, it can most likely be found in there.

A movement to my right makes me start. A group of spooky characters walks by a few blocks from me. They look like a hybrid of zombies and walking pigs, and that's exactly what they are: zombie pigmen. They carry swords, but normally they're harmless. As long as I don't attack them, they will remain peaceful – at least in the real game. How they'll react in this subconscious world, I'm not eager to explore. So I carry on as fast as I can.

Soon I reach the outskirts of the fortress. It looks like a city on stilts after a bombing raid. Large columns of reddish-black nether bricks rise up from the lava. Their tops are connected by narrow walkways with box-shaped buildings in between.

On its giant pillars, right in the middle of the lake, the fortress seems out of reach. But I'm in the Cubeworld after all, so I just take a few dozen blocks of the reddish netherrack that's the common building material down here and craft my own column beneath me, until I am at the level of the walkways. Now I only have to carefully glue some blocks to the column right before me, edging myself forward over the lava lake.

This works just fine, until a ghastly wailing makes me turn around. One of the nasty fire breathers approaches me.

Now I'm in trouble. While it was relatively easy to dodge the fireballs on the ground, up here my mobility is very limited. Even worse, if a fireball hits the improvised bridge made of netherrack, it will certainly be destroyed and I'll take a swim in the lava lake. I can still try to play fireball tennis like before, but a single mistake would be my end.

I try to close the gap between the fortress and me as quickly as possible. There are only two blocks missing when I hear the roar of a fireball behind me.

My only chance is to cross the gap with a courageous jump onto the edge of the fortress. But the gap looks damn wide to me.

There's no time to think. Just as I jump, the fireball hits the self-constructed bridge behind me, leaving only a few burning blocks hanging in thin air.

I feel the force of the blow in my back. My health sinks down to almost zero.

With a little help from the force of the explosion, I manage to land on the edge of the fortress. For a moment, everything goes black. I feel as if I'm losing my balance, falling backward into the glowing depth. But I regain my feet just in time.

The ghast wails in disappointment, preparing for the next attack.

I don't wait for it. Instead, I run toward the covered part of the fortress as fast as I can. Behind me, another fireball explodes, without doing much damage.

I manage to enter the comparative safety of the black walls. Here, I'm out of reach of the ghast's fireballs. But in a Nether fortress, there are worse things to be expected.

I drink a potion of healing, eat some bread, and rest for a while, before I start exploring the fortress.

I follow a roofed corridor. Through windows in the walls, I can see the cave outside, lit by the lava lake and glowstone. I hear the ghast wailing, but I don't see it.

Soon I reach a larger complex of buildings. I enter a room with a lava well bubbling in the middle. Three corridors set off from here.

The passageway opposite of me is guarded by a single zombie pigman with a sword. Motionless, he stares at me with empty eyes. This is unusual: zombie pigmen usually wander about in small groups. This one, however, looks like he has a purpose - guarding the passage. There's certainly a reason for that.

I approach the guard. His head follows every move I make.

"Please, let me pass," I say.

The zombie pigman grunts something incomprehensible to me.

I already went through this before. I grunt something back. The undead pigman answers. Unfortunately, I don't understand a word. The result, however, is unmistakable: He stands his ground.

Words, or grunts, obviously will not achieve anything. Attacking the guard seems to be the only option. But I hesitate. I can easily deal with one of them. But if you attack one, then all of them act hostile to you, at least all in the vicinity. I can't see or hear other zombie pigmen, but that doesn't mean one or more aren't somewhere nearby.

I better avoid any unnecessary risk. So instead I follow the path to the left. After a while, it opens onto an open platform. As I step on it, I hear the ghast wailing not far away. Quickly, I draw back into the protection of the walls, following the corridor in the opposite direction.

Shortly after the room with the guard, the corridor turns left. Maybe I can get around the guard this way.

Soon I step into another room with four exits. The passage to the left is guarded by another zombie pigman.

Obviously, there's an inner area of the fortress, which is guarded by the undead. I know my subconscious well enough by now to gather that that's exactly where I must go. Still, I continue exploring the other passages. As expected, they lead to dead ends.

I return to the second guard. Again, he won't budge, regardless of my attempts to speak zombie-pigmanish.

But maybe there's another peaceful solution. I attack the wall next to the passage with my diamond pickaxe.

The guard utters a grunt that sounds unmistakably like a warning.

I ignore it. I never heard of a zombie pigman acting aggressively on his own, without being attacked first.

I remove a few blocks of nether brick next to the guard. He grunts threateningly, but he doesn't attack. Behind him, there's another room with four exits, lit by torches. There are pictures on the walls showing strange symbols that I have never seen before.

I move past the guard toward the staircase that leads down in the center of the room.

As soon as I step into the room, the undead creature lets out an eerie squeal, as if a pig has been slaughtered. The next instant, I feel an electrical shock in my back. The zombie pigman has attacked!

I turn around to fend off the attack, but more zombie pigmen pour into the room from the other exits and the stairwell. Within moments, I'm surrounded. Their swords lash at me rapidly. I barely have time to utter, "I'm sorry, I just wanted ..." before everything fades to black.

So that's it.

18.

Something is wrong. Something is very wrong with this world.

The world is a large room with walls made of reddish-black nether bricks, lit by the glow of lava that's bubbling in four basins in the corners. Pictures of strange symbols adorn the walls. One of them depicts a stylized flame with eyes and a mouth. In the middle of the room is an altar made of obsidian, and I am lying on it.

I am surrounded by figures clad in long, dark red robes, the hoods casting deep shades over their faces. They grunt rhythmically, as if they are a herd of pigs trying to perform a monk's choral.

Whatever's going on here, it hasn't much similarity to what normally happens in the computer game Minecraft.

Apparently, I didn't die, or I'd have respawned in Simon's bed. Maybe I was unconscious for a few minutes while the zombie pigmen carried me into their temple, or whatever this is.

I try to get up, but I can't move. Am I paralyzed? No, I can see that my arms and legs have been tied to the altar.

The zombie pigmen step aside and bow to a strange figure that now enters the room. It is an enderman, but he's wearing a white doctor's coat.

He bends over me. His cold eyes regard me. "I'm sorry, Marco," he whispers. "You shouldn't have interfered!"

No! I want to shout. No, please, just give me one last chance! But no sound escapes my throat.

The enderman holds something in his tentacle-like arm, something long and sharp. A dagger? No, even worse: a syringe.

"Don't worry, it won't hurt," he breathes. "You're just going to fall asleep and ..."

I can hear footsteps approaching. The enderman freezes, then moves his head, as if listening. Quickly, he hides the syringe within his white coat.

A female voice that sounds as if it is coming from very far away, and very close at the same time, says "Who are you? What are you doing here? Visiting hours are long over!"

The room flickers, as if it were some kind of slowly dissolving mirage. The zombie pigmen disappear. The enderman transforms into Amely's stepfather. He doesn't wear a doctor's coat, but jeans, a light blue shirt, and a gray jacket. His left hand is hiding something in his pocket.

"I just wanted to have another look at the boy," he explains. "I'm a doctor."

"You are the one who called the ambulance?" I can see the nurse only out of the corner of my eye. She has gray hair tied in a bun.

"Yes."

Her voice is determined. "The boy's medical treatment is now the responsibility of Dr. Berkholm. If you want to discuss it with him, you should ask for an appointment. And now please leave, for I need to wash the patient."

"Yes, of course." Amely's stepfather says in an almost submissive tone, which must be hard for him. "I'm sorry."

I sink backwards into a deep, black well. I try to hold on to reality, but I can find no grip. No sound escapes my throat.

I'm back in the Nether fortress. The zombie pigmen are there, grunting excitedly. The enderman is gone.

The nurse saved my life. But Amely's stepfather will be

back, that much is clear. The danger is only temporarily averted.

One of the undead creatures bends over me. He makes grunting noises. Only after a moment do I realize they are sounding similar to human words. "What ... you ... do?"

"I ... I didn't do anything!" I say.

"High priest gone!" the zombie pigman grunts. "You did away!"

The others shriek at each other, as if they're fighting.

"Let me go!" I say.

"No," the zombie pigman who can speak human says. "High priest gone! Big disaster! Fire god mad! We must calm! Must give sacrifice!"

"Sacrifice!" The others imitate the word more or less recognizably. "Sacrifice! Sacrifice!"

"Shut up!" I shout.

The zombie pigmen fall silent.

"You've got the wrong guy! I am a warrior of the fire god! You can't sacrifice me!"

"You lying!" the zombie pigman says. He seems to be their leader, at least as long as the enderman isn't around. "High priest says you traitor!"

"The high priest is lying!" I shout. "Let me up, and I'll prove it to you!"

The undead shriek at each other. Finally, they untie me.

"You go in room of fire god," the leader says. "If you live, we believe you say truth. If you dead, we sacrifice. Fire god happy both ways!"

The room of the fire god? If that's a place with a floor of lava, I'm a goner. But I have no choice but to go on with my pretense, if I don't want to die here and now.

"All right, lead me to the room of the fire god!" I say.

The zombie pigmen start chanting rhythmically. They drag me out of the room and down a long corridor that ends in another room. In the middle is a lava well. The walls are decorated with the strange flame face I saw before. In the opposite wall is a steel door with a button next to it.

The leader presses the button. The door swings open, revealing a short corridor with another steel door at the end. Like an airlock.

"That way to room of fire god," the leader explains. "You go in!"

It's obvious what's going to happen: As soon as I close the first door, the second one will open. There will probably be no button on the inside. No way out but stepping through the second door into whatever lies beyond. It's going to be unpleasant, that's for sure.

The only way out of this room leads back to the altar. I could try to dig myself through the walls, but the zombie pigmen would probably object. In a fight, I wouldn't stand a chance against them.

So there's nothing left to do but follow the order. The monks grunt a rhythmic chant as I walk through the door with my head held high.

With a click, the door closes behind me. At the same instant, the other one opens. It leads to a large room made of Nether bricks with a low ceiling. For the most part, the floor consists of lava. There is a small island of obsidian blocks in the middle, and some single obsidian blocks scattered around the floor. I recognize this kind of challenge: In order to reach the safe spot, you have to jump from one block to the next without slipping and falling into the lava.

Unfortunately, matters are made difficult by a cage sitting on the island in the middle with a fire burning inside it. It's a spawner.

The monsters it creates each have a large flaming head that floats in the air, with a number of white-hot rods spinning around it at high speed. These look like fuel rods in a nuclear power plant.

Blazes. Pretty nasty foes.

Two of them are floating above the lava toward me. They make noises as if breathing in deeply, then each shoots three fireballs at me in quick succession.

You cannot deflect a blaze fireball with a sword. No Andre Agassi tactics this time. My only chance is to dodge them. But that is far from easy if you're trapped in a narrow corridor. All I can do is run toward them and try to jump on the next obsidian block.

One of the fiery missiles grazes my left arm, creating a sharp pain that spreads into my chest.

Ouch! That hurt!

The blazes, now positioned on both sides of the entrance, inhale deeply. I jump on an adjacent obsidian block. But I have too much forward momentum and almost slip over the edge. With flailing arms, I barely manage to keep my balance.

The blaze fireballs have missed me this time, but the monsters are repositioning themselves for the next attack.

I use the brief pause to make two more jumps, reaching the island in the middle of the room. I could try to destroy the spawner cage, but that takes time, and I'd be defenseless against the attacks.

Zwoosh ... a burst of fireballs shoots at me. I jump aside, but one of them hits my leg, which bursts into flame.

I feel terrible pain, as if I really was burning alive. In vain, I try to extinguish the flames.

Again, the blazes inhale.

I can't do anything but try to escape their next attack, in the hopes that the flames on my leg will die out on their own. If only the pain wasn't so terrible! Colorful spots dance before my eyes.

I can't give up now!

I exchange the sword in my hand for bow and arrows, the most effective weapon against blazes. Fortunately, there were lots of arrows in the chest in the zombie home. I shoot an arrow, but miss. It gets stuck in the wall near one of the monsters.

Again, the blazes shoot their charges at me. I manage to dodge them, at the same time hitting one of the monsters with an arrow. It makes a sound like the clanging of metal.

The hit raises my spirits. Blazes are tough, but not invincible. But just as I aim the next arrow, I feel a searing pain in my back. I turn around. A third blaze has spawned behind me. Now I'm surrounded. They fire at me from three sides at once.

I stand no chance against them. Even if I managed to kill one of them, another one would simply spawn.

I'm dead. I could as well jump into the lava.

A volley of fireballs hits me, three in a row. The pain is cruel, as if a dentist is drilling directly into a nerve without any anesthesia.

Why does this hurt so much? Up until now, a hit felt like a weak electroshock. Does the pain signal that these fireballs are doing even more damage? But why am I not dead, then?

Wait a minute! My body is literally in flames, but my

health is still at its maximum! The fireballs hurt like hell, but they do no real damage.

If only they weren't so painful!

I force myself to just stand, accepting the pain. I make my body rigid, while one round of fireballs after another hits me.

I black out.

I am back in the hospital room. It is dark, apart from the soft glow of LEDs beside my bed.

My body burns. At least if feels like it. I groan with pain.

Yes, I really did groan!

What's happening? Is the pain indicating a deterioration of my condition?

Maybe it's just the opposite! Pain is a signal from the body to the brain. That I can feel the pain means that a part of the communication is working!

I try to groan again, but I'm already sinking back into the tunnel.

The blazes buzz around me, firing at me like maniacs. Apparently, they're unable to do anything else.

After a while, the intensity of the pain diminishes, as if my nerves have grown tired. Maybe I'm just getting used to it.

Ignoring the blazes, I look around. On the wall opposite of the entrance, there's a lever. It will probably open the door at the end of the corridor.

I jump from block to block. The blazes continue to buzz around me like mad hornets. They are irritating, but not really dangerous.

I reach the lever, pulling it down.

Immediately the blazes cease their attacks. The door at the end of the corridor opens. I can hear excited squeals and grunts. Some of the zombie pigmen approach down the corridor, stopping at the edge of the lava. They stare at me in disbelief.

I jump toward them, trying not to let them see my pain. The flames on my body start to extinguish by themselves, but it still hurts like hell.

The undead chant rhythmically as they escort me to the outside. In the anteroom, they bow their heads to me.

"You say truth," the leader exclaims. "You big warrior of fire god. You now our high priest!"

"I cannot stay with you," I answer. "I need to fulfill a quest."

"We help you with quest. We go wherever you go. Even to Overworld, if need be."

"That's very decent of you. Maybe you can really help me. I need to find the exit."

The grunts die down. The zombie pigmen stare at me from beneath their hoods. For a moment, I'm afraid I have made them angry again.

But the voice of the leader is full of awe as he asks, "You want go to exit?"

"Yes. Do you know where it is?"

"We know. But not good place. Evil things there."

What a surprise! "Where is it?"

The undead creature points down. "Is deep in soil. Below lava lake. We cannot go there. We can only show gate."

"Agreed," I say.

The zombie pigmen bow their heads once more. Then they lead me down the corridor toward the altar room, and from there through a labyrinth of corridors and staircases until we reach a small, square room. In the middle, there's a hole in the floor, just one block wide. I bend over it, but can't see anything but blackness.

"This gate to exit," the leader says.

I listen, but I can't hear the typical humming of a Nether portal, nor any other sound. The hole just seems to lead into nothingness.

"Are you sure this is the exit?" I ask.

The zombie pigman shakes his head. "This not exit. This gate to exit."

"I don't understand."

"You go through gate. Then dark corridors. Evil things. There exit. Is guarded by god of darkness."

A shiver runs down my spine. My whole body still hurts, even if the pain has dulled. And now I'm supposed to jump into a dark shaft? Could it be a ruse by the zombie pigmen? Maybe they're afraid of me and want to get rid of me this way.

"Many went in there," the leader explains. "None back. We not go there."

"How do you know what's down there, then?"

"It says in book of gods."

Zombie pigmen who read! The Cubeworld is full of surprises.

"We cannot defeat evil creatures of god of darkness. But you big warrior of fire god. You can defeat!"

The other monks make encouraging grunts. They really seem to believe that I'm some kind of mystic hero from their legends. I, on the other hand, feel like a steak that's just been put through a meat grinder and then grilled on charcoal, well done. Only the ketchup is missing.

"You not want go exit?" the leader asks. "You want stay with us, be our high priest?"

This hopeful question convinces me that he told me the truth, or at least what he believes to be the truth.

"I'd love to. But I'm afraid I must go down there. Thanks for your help!"

The zombie pigmen bow their heads one last time, chanting their grunted choral.

I take a deep breath, take a step forward, and plunge down into the darkness.

19

I fall, fall, fall. The shaft seems to be endless. I try to concentrate on the hospital room. If I could only wake up for good, I wouldn't have to deal with all the dangers of the Cubeworld anymore.

At this point, though, I almost wish a monster would attack me. The pain would help me connect to my body. But all I can feel is a cool wind coming up from below while I fall into absolute blackness.

Splash! I land in water. Apparently, I have jumped into an ordinary well, if a very deep one.

I flail my arms and legs, trying to get to the surface, but a strong current pulls me deeper. Wouldn't it be ironic if I ended up drowning in this well that I stupidly jumped into?

Suddenly, a bluish glow surrounds me. As I thrash around, my head breaks the surface. I take a deep breath. But I'm still falling, part of a seemingly endless waterfall.

Another splash as I land in a wider body of water. This time, I manage to get to the surface.

I'm swimming in a lake at the bottom of an enormous cave. As far as I can see, its walls are not made of netherrack, but of dark stone - probably bedrock. Clusters of glowing cubes on the ceiling emit a soft light. They look like glowstone, but they gleam blue instead of yellow.

The waterfall I came through pours down from the ceiling high above.

I paddle to the shore of the lake. I can hear nothing but the lapping of water and a very soft beeping sound. This encourages me. It sounds like the medical instruments beside my bed. Maybe I'm close to waking up!

The sound seems to come from an elongated part of the

cave. I walk toward it.

The cave narrows until it is not much more than a tube winding through the rock like intestines made of stone.

I look down at my diamond sword, which shines in the bluish glow like Frodo Baggins's Sting right before an orc attack. So far, I haven't encountered any creatures, but that doesn't mean anything. The zombie pigmen's warnings were clear, and I have no reason not to take them seriously.

The cave takes another turn before it widens into a large room. At its end sits a giant skull, its eyes glowing blue. The toothless mouth is wide open, as if he's laughing hard. Behind it, an unlit passageway seems to lead onward.

My subconscious obviously tends to be a bit melodramatic.

Without hesitation, I step through the open mouth.

Darkness engulfs me like a black, gooey liquid, blocking all my senses. The beeping noise gets even quieter, until I can't hear it at all.

I move on, without knowing whether I really make any progress.

After what seems an endless time, I see a soft bluish glow before me. I come into another room made of black stone. In regular intervals, blue glowstones are set into the walls. It looks like a part of an underground fortress.

At the far end of the room, the passageway continues. To the left and right of the passageway, two skeletons stand. They are unusually large, their bones blackened as if burned. Unlike normal Minecraft skeletons, they carry swords instead of bows.

Wither skeletons! I have heard of these mobs but I have never encountered them in the game. But I do know that they are much stronger than their Overworld cousins.

The monsters regard me with empty eyes, then run at me, swords raised high. I shoot a few arrows at them, then I draw my own sword as they come into reach.

Soon, I'm tied up in a heavy fight. Wither skeletons are tough and strong. Even worse, each time they hit me, I black out for a brief moment, so I have a hard time keeping my balance and direction. At the same time, they seem to heal themselves with the life energy they drain from me. If it weren't for my supply of potions of healing, I'd be dead already.

I change my tactics. Instead of dividing my attention between both foes, I focus on one, ignoring the other. As a result, I take a quick succession of hits, my life energy dwindling down rapidly. But I manage to destroy one of the skeletons. It dissolves in a cloud of smoke, leaving its cubic skull behind.

Now it's easier to defend myself against the other one. After a brief, but heavy fight, it goes down as well.

I gather the two skulls. You never know when a wither skeleton skull might come in handy. It sure would look nice on the bookshelf in my room.

Did I really think that? Am I so confused as to believe I can take items from my dream world back to reality?

I shake my head. If I can't find the exit soon, I'll probably lose my mind.

I walk into the passageway. As I suspected, it is the entrance to a large subterranean fortress. The corridor turns right and leads to a junction. There, after hesitating briefly, I turn left, in the direction that I presume will lead me deeper inside.

Again, the passage turns to the right, then to the left, and again to the left, until it ends in another junction.

I turn right. This time, the passage leads straight to the next junction.

I stray from passage to passage, from junction to junction. I try to head to where I think I should go, but soon I have lost any sense of direction. This obviously is some kind of labyrinth.

After a while, I pause. I have randomly chosen the last few turns and have no idea at all which way I should go.

I get hungry and eat two loaves of bread. They taste dry, but they give me an idea.

I drop another loaf of bread, leaving it hovering above the black floor. I randomly choose an exit. The passage turns left and leads to another junction.

In the middle, there's a loaf of bread.

Dammit! This can't be! The passage only made one turn, so it cannot lead back to the place I came from in a loop. But apparently I have come back to my starting point anyway.

I try another passage. This leads straight to another junction, with bread.

I turn around, following the passageway back. Although it was straight when I came here, it now makes a turn to the right. I'm not at all surprised to find a loaf of bread at the next junction.

My subconscious is playing unfair!

I gather the bread. This way, I'll get nowhere.

I examine the four passages leaving this place. But as hard as I try, I see no difference between them. I look closely at one of the blocks they are made from. Its surface is smooth, painted with little squares in different dark gray tones. Graphic pixels. They look like a mosaic that's supposed to depict a stone block.

I compare various blocks, but they look identical.

I listen in the hopes of hearing the soft beep of the medical instruments beside my bed. But I can't hear anything at all – not even the sound of my own breathing.

"Hello?" I shout. My voice sounds dry and weak, as if the walls have absorbed the sound.

I get uneasy. I am lost somewhere in the depths of my own mind. How can I ever find the way out?

Standing around won't get me anywhere. I take a left into a passage that turns to the right after a few steps.

I stop in my tracks. Why did I choose this passage? Why not one of the others? Was my choice really random?

I go back to the junction, waiting a moment. I think of Amely. I realize that I never saw her smile, let alone laugh. What wouldn't I do to paint a little joy on her face!

I sigh, moving on. Without thinking, I take the same passage as before. Again, I stop.

There's something wrong here!

I go back to the junction and look in all four directions. The passageway I took before somehow feels right. No, not right. Safe.

The longer I think about it, the stronger the feeling gets: The passageway I just came from is the best choice. In the other directions lies danger.

Unconsciously, I avoided that danger. I took the path of least resistance.

I regard the other passages, trying to sense what kinds of nasty surprises they may hold for me.

The passage straight ahead seems to be the most dangerous.

I gather my courage and walk into it.

Again, I reach a junction. This time, I sense clearly that

the safest route is to go back the way I came. I feel a strong urge to turn around and look for a safe path.

The passage to the left and the one straight ahead appear threatening. The passage to the right makes me afraid.

I take the right passageway.

This one turns left. Behind the corner, I run into a wither skeleton that has been lying in wait for me. Before I can react, it hits me. A strong electrical shock surges through my body, draining my life energy.

I feel an overwhelming urge to turn and run. These wither skeletons are much too strong as foes!

I pull myself together, draw my sword, and attack my adversary with all my might.

The fight goes back and forth. My fear seems to encumber me, slowing down my movements, as if I had taken sleeping pills. Again and again, the skeleton strikes me, drawing from my life energy to heal the damage I just inflicted on it. My supply of potions of healing diminishes quickly.

I realize that I can't defeat the wither skeleton. It will kill me, and then everything is lost. Better I give up and flee before it is too late!

"No!" I shout at myself. "Think of Amely, stupid!"

Indeed, the thought gives me strength. My movements become faster, more coordinated. With a quick combination of sword swings, I hit the skeleton three times. It crumbles, leaving only its head behind.

I pick it up and continue my way through the labyrinth.

At the next junction, it's the passage to the left that frightens me most. For a long time, I just stare at it. This time, there won't be only one skeleton waiting for me, I'm sure. Maybe I should try one of the other passages first. After all, they look pretty dangerous too.

No! My fear leads me. It's like I have to swim against a strong current in order to reach the source of a river.

Still, it takes me a long time before I overcome my fear and enter the passage to the left. The thought of what awaits me at its end frightens me more and more. I must force myself to take each single step. Again and again, I stop, fighting the urge to turn back. It's not too late yet, my fear shouts at me. You still can get back to safety!

The passage turns right. Cautiously, I peer around the corner, expecting to see a whole horde of wither skeletons, ready to jump upon me and hack me to pieces within seconds. But the passage is empty.

I feel no relief. Quite the opposite: I know that whatever comes next will be even worse than a horde of wither skeletons.

I feel as if cold sweat is breaking from each and every pore, although my body doesn't even have pores. I tremble, my heartbeat fluttering.

I realize that I've been standing rooted to the spot for some time. I focus on the task of telling my legs to move forward. They comply only reluctantly.

Finally, I reach the end of the passage. It leads into a square room three blocks in size. Passages lead in all four directions, all emanating an aura of deadly danger. But that's nothing compared to the feeling I get when I look at the fifth exit: a square, black hole in the middle of the room.

The idea of jumping into it, throwing myself into the darkness, the unknown, makes me panic. It would be sure death.

"No!" I exclaim. "Anything but this! I don't want to go in there!"

But if I want to follow the trace of my fear, that is exactly what I need to do.

Paralyzed, I stand at the edge of the hole. I force myself to look down into it. I can see nothing but blackness.

Is that the exit? Am I just a step away from waking up?

No, my fear cries. It would be a terrible mistake to jump in there!

I stop, looking around in confusion. I'm back at one of the junctions I passed earlier, a hole in the floor nowhere in sight. Apparently I ran here without even realizing it.

I turn around. The passage behind me looms like the gaping mouth of a giant reptile.

I can't do that! I can't go back to the room with the hole again! I wouldn't be able to stand looking at it. The thought that I could take a wrong step and accidently fall into it makes me sick. Never, ever would I jump in there on purpose!

I take a deep breath. Think of Amely!

I picture her as she stood at the edge of the schoolyard, eyes cast down. How frightened she must have been! How difficult it must have been for her to open up to me! Compared to what she went through, my task is easy!

I turn and follow the path. As I enter the room with the hole, I don't look at it. I just stare straight ahead and walk on, until I step into nothing.

I tumble down into the shaft. I want to cry out, but fear chokes me.

20.

I fall, fall, fall. The shaft seems to be endless. Absolute darkness engulfs me. I try to hear beeping, but there's nothing.

I'm going to fall forever! Jumping into the shaft was the worst mistake I ever made. Why didn't I listen to the warnings of my subconscious?

Suddenly, there's light. I fall through an opening in the ceiling of a giant room, lit by blue glowstones.

There's no water below me, just the naked stone floor.

With a dull thud, I crash onto it. I fade out for a moment. My health is at a minimum.

I gather myself up and look around. The room is at least fifty blocks high. It's a wonder that I survived the fall. As far as I can see, there are giant stone pillars reaching up to the ceiling, each four blocks in diameter and made of indestructible bedrock. The light of the glowstones far above barely reaches the floor.

I'm cold.

I drink a potion of healing. My health increases, but I still feel weak.

I wander around among the columns. They seem to stretch out endlessly in all directions like a giant stone forest, faintly glowing in the bluish light as if bathed in moonshine. I try to feel which direction frightens me most, but the sense of danger is the same wherever I turn. Once in a while, I discover patches of brown-gray sand in the stone floor. As I look closer, I perceive vague faces, their mouths open as if crying in pain. Soul sand! A deep sadness befalls me as I look at them, making my shoulders sag, slowing down my steps.

I turn away and avoid the patches as much as I can.

I wander on aimlessly while my desperation grows. Whatever I have achieved in the Cubeworld has only led to something worse. I'll never find a way out of here, and if I do, it will only be jumping out of the frying pan into the fire.

Suddenly, I see something lying on the floor in the distance. My heart beats faster. There are objects lying there!

I run toward them. But as I recognize what I see, I stop in my tracks.

A heap of things hovers over the floor near a pillar: a sword and diamond armor, potions of healing, provisions, tools, materials of all kinds – all the things that I carry with me. It's as if this stack is an exact duplicate of the contents in my mind.

With horror, I realize what this means. If you die in the computer game Minecraft, you awake at the point where you last slept. But all the items you carry remain at the place where you died.

I've been here before!

I remember finding myself on a beach, without memories, but with a strong feeling that something was wrong with the world. How often did that happen? How often have I been pursued in the desert by zombies and creepers? How often did I meet Simon, fight the enderman, solve the puzzles in the room with the levers? How often did I get back my memories, only to lose them again in the end? How often did I conquer my fear, only to end up in this endless hall?

I wander on. It doesn't take long until I find another stack of items. And soon after, another.

Now it is obvious that there is no exit. I will wander around here forever, until I die of exhaustion. Then another stack of items will document my futile attempts to escape the Cubeworld.

I wonder what would have happened if I had followed Simon's advice and gone through the End portal. But what use is such speculation? Apparently, I have made the same mistake over and over again. Otherwise I wouldn't be here.

As I encounter the fifth stack of items, I examine them more closely. There are more than enough bread loaves and potions of healing. So I will not starve anytime soon.

How did I die, then?

Startled, I look around me. Was there a movement in the shadows between the columns?

I must have been mistaken. I turn my attention to the stack again. It seems to be an exact copy of the contents of my mind. The only things missing are the three wither skeleton skulls.

Now I know what killed me.

For me, the Wither is more a legend than reality. I have never seen one and know no one who encountered one, much less survived the encounter.

What I know is this: A Wither doesn't appear on its own. You have to summon it. For that, you need four blocks of soul sand and three skulls of wither skeletons. You arrange the soul sand in the shape of a T, put the three skulls on top of it, and *shazam*, the Wither materializes in front of you! Why anyone would be stupid enough to follow this recipe has never occurred to me.

But apparently, I have done this before. More than once. Maybe a dozen times. Or hundreds of times?

The thought makes me shudder.

I turn away from the stack. There must be another way!

There isn't. I try to dig into the floor, walls, and even the ceiling with my tools, but it's no use. I can only dig up the soul sand.

As I take one cube of it into my mind, I get in such a depressed mood that I spit it out again quickly. Below the patch of sand, there's only indestructible bedrock.

I realize I have only two options: I can walk around here until my supplies are used up and even the remains of my former tries reveal no more food. Or I can confront the inescapable here and now. But the idea of creating the Wither, which in all likelihood will kill me, takes away all my courage.

Think of Amely!

She must feel like I do now, trapped in an inescapable situation. If I can't wake up and make the truth about her stepfather known, she will be snared in eternal darkness, just like me.

Even if I have to die a hundred times over, I will try to help her again and again!

I overcome my aversion and collect four blocks of soul sand, which I stack in the shape of a T. I place the three skulls on top of the upper three blocks.

As soon as I put down the last skull, the whole arrangement starts to grow, flashing in a blue light. The Wither awakes!

I run away. From behind a pillar at a safe distance, I watch what's happening.

With a thundering explosion, the Wither comes to life. It has a torso of dark bones like the skeletons, but no arms or legs. It hovers above the ground. Its three heads turn, searching.

So far, it hasn't discovered me, so it remains nonaggressive. But if I wanted to hide from it, I shouldn't have created it in the first place! I assume that I must destroy it to somehow escape its domain.

I shoot a well-aimed arrow. It hits, doing little damage. But now the Wither has noticed me. It shoots missiles from its three heads in different directions. One flies over my head, hits a pillar, and rolls along the floor behind me. It's a wither skeleton skull.

I shoot another arrow, hitting the Wither. It shoots back, but even though it can shoot three skulls at once, I find it relatively easy to dodge them.

Arrow after arrow hits my enemy, while skull after skull misses me. Hope rises in me. Can it be so easy to defeat the legendary monster?

From the corner of my eye, I detect a movement. Between two pillars, out of reach of my bow, a single enderman stands, regarding me silently. He wears a white coat.

All right, I can take on this scumbag any time. "Come closer, if you dare!" I shout.

But the enderman doesn't move. Even as I turn away my gaze, he doesn't attack.

A hit in the back makes me jump. I hadn't been watching the Wither, which hit me with a skull. I lose some life energy, which it devours greedily.

I shoot another arrow at it, and another, while I dodge its attacks.

Again, something hits me in the back.

I spin around, convinced that the devious enderman has snuck up on me. Instead, a wither skeleton stands before me. Where did that come from?

While I parry its next attack, I see one of the skulls that the Wither shoots rolling over the floor. It ends up on a patch of soul sand. At the next instant, it rises up, carried by a skeletal body that steps out of the sand patch like a dead man from his grave.

I look around, discovering to my horror that in this way, already half a dozen wither skeletons have been created. They close in on me from all sides, while the Wither shoots volley after volley of skulls.

The enderman regards me without emotion, like a spectator at a boxing match, the result of which is determined from the beginning. There seems to be something like regret in his fiery stare.

I fight my way to a column and position myself with my back to it. In this way, I am protected against attacks from behind. But at the same time, I cannot dodge attacks very well anymore. Quickly, my life energy diminishes while even more wither skeletons appear around me.

Now I remember that all the stacks of items where always lying next to a pillar. Maybe it wasn't such a brilliant idea to position myself with my back to it, closing off any route of escape.

The stacks. Something is wrong with them.

I don't know where that thought comes from, or what it means, but I try to cling to it, while sword strokes pelt me from all sides.

I drink a potion of healing, but its effect is diminished quickly by the ceaseless attacks from the skeletons. They drain my life energy faster than I can heal myself. It's only a matter of moments before they put me out of my miserable existence. Then I'll find myself at the edge of a cubic sea, wondering what's wrong with the world.

Wait a minute! Shouldn't I have seen traces of my earlier attempts in the Cubeworld? Shouldn't there have been a hole in the ground in the desert where a creeper exploded? Shouldn't I have found the huts I constructed earlier?

But there was nothing like that.

If there really were earlier attempts of mine to leave the Cubeworld, everything was erased when I failed. Otherwise, Simon wouldn't have been so surprised to see me, and the door in the room with the levers would have stood open.

So if the Cubeworld is reset after every failed attempt, then there can't be any traces of me being in this hall before!

Finally, I realize what's going on: The stacks of items lying around here are only to convince me that I have tried in vain to escape a hundred times before. They are designed to rob me of my hopes and my willpower. They are nothing than a giant bluff! And I fell for it!

The thought makes me incredibly angry.

I slash with my sword like a berserker. The wither skeletons shatter under my sword strokes as if their bones were made of glass. Soon, I'm surrounded only by a pile of bones.

The Wither continues to shoot skulls, but most of them tumble around harmlessly. If one of them drops onto soul sand, I destroy the skeleton before it even rises to its full height.

It's time to deal with the main culprit. With a few strides, I close in on it.

It turns its heads toward me and shoots a skull right in my face.

A searing pain hits me. I black out for a second.

I can hear the beeping of the medical instruments. The picture of the dark hospital room mixes with the pillars.

I am not alone!

Someone stands beside me, motionless. Since I can't turn my head, I can see him only out of the corner of my eye. He wears a white coat.

Before I can make out more details, I sink back down the tunnel.

I reach the Cubeworld just in time. My health is close to zero.

I attack the Wither with fast strokes. As I am about to finish it off, there's an ugly cracking sound, and the sword in my hand disappears.

Dammit! Of all times for my weapon to wear out and break! I don't have another diamond sword. I could run away and find one in one of the stacks, but in the meantime, the Wither would create a fresh army of skeletons.

I make a wide swing with my arm, landing a nasty uppercut to one of the skulls. It disconnects from the body, flying through the air to tumble across the floor.

Why didn't I think of this before?

In no time I have dislodged the other two heads. The Wither crumbles into a pile of soul sand.

I look around. The wither skulls lying around disappear one after another with a soft plop, until the last traces of the fight have vanished.

I finally overcame even this danger. But what for? I'm still standing in the hall of pillars. There's no exit to be seen anywhere.

"I'm sorry, Marco!" someone whispers behind me.

Startled, I turn around.

The enderman has snuck up on me. He holds something – a small, rectangular syringe.

"Get lost!" I shout.

Ignoring me, he reaches out for my left arm. I want to run away, but my legs are rooted to the ground. As I look down, I see that I'm standing on a patch of soul sand. My legs have sunk into it a little. The tortured souls in the sand seem to cling to them, as if trying to pull me down.

"Don't be afraid, it won't hurt!" the enderman whispers. Only it isn't the enderman. It is Amely's stepfather, bending down over me. I can smell alcohol on his breath. His face seems distorted in pain, as if he's really sorry about me. But his eyes gleam coldly.

I try to defend myself, but my body is still paralyzed. I can do nothing but watch him with wide-open eyes.

As the needle penetrates my arm, a wave of pain washes over me. I make an inaudible cry.

"Good night, Marco!" the enderman whispers.

The pillars around me begin to transform. Their sharp edges become soft and round, their flat bases beginning to swell. They are melting!

The whole giant room dissolves. Black liquid drops down from the ceiling, seeps out of the lower ends of the pillars, gushes up from the patches of soul sand. It flows around my legs that are still trapped.

The enderman laughs hoarsely, then vanishes.

The black flood rises higher and higher. It reaches my chest, my shoulders. I let out a last, desperate cry before the bitter liquid fills my mouth and lungs.

Again, darkness engulfs me. Only a soft beeping sound disrupts the silence. It gets fainter, until it dies away.

21

Darkness. Emptiness. Silence. Is this the end?

Even the question seems strange. Why am I able to ask it at all?

Apparently, I'm not dead. Not yet.

Or is this the afterlife? Will I be forever suspended weightlessly in this endless darkness?

But the emptiness is not absolute. There is something: a tiny, pale spot, infinitely far away.

The spot grows into an irregular, gray-green patch.

I'm falling toward it.

Soon, the patch fills my field of vision. Now I recognize it: an island, hovering in nothingness. Pillars of obsidian reach up to me, each crowned with a shining crystal. Black figures with glowing eyes look up at me, while I tumble down toward them.

I have come to the End.

I hit the floor. A shock runs through me. I drink a potion of healing, but I can feel my life energy seeping away, even though I am not under attack. Something inside me drains my health.

The syringe. Amely's stepfather injected something into me. Maybe an overdose of a sleep-inducing drug.

He's clever. It will take a while until the pulsing curve of my heartbeat will go flat and the appliances beside my bed will trigger an alarm.

He'll have more than enough time to leave the hospital, unrecognized.

I must wake up! Now!

But I am trapped here in the End. The only way out is by defeating the terrible Enderdragon.

Endermen stand around me. They look around, searching, as if they can sense my presence but can't see me. I carefully avoid looking into their eyes.

Suddenly, I hear the rustle of leathery wings. He's coming for me!

The Enderdragon is huge. His cold, glowing eyes glare as he elegantly winds around an obsidian pillar and rushes toward me.

I can't help but admire his beauty. The pale light gleams on his black scales. His body moves through the air in graceful waves.

Like an arrow he dashes at me. His small head hits my breast. Something breaks within me.

I'm hurled through the air, landing a few blocks away. The dragon flies over me, cycling up into the dark sky, only to turn on me again.

The endermen stand silently, watching my desperate fight for survival.

Again the dragon shoots down at me. I throw myself to the side, barely escaping the attack. I manage to hit him with an arrow. But as soon as he flies past one of the pillars, glowing spots emanate from the crystal on top of it, healing its wound.

If I am to kill the dragon, I need to destroy those crystals first. But I can never manage that. I've only got a few dozen arrows - too few to survive this fight. On top of that, the potions of healing seem to have little effect against the slow dissipation of my health.

A flash of memory comes from somewhere deep inside me. It seems as appropriate to my situation as a clown's nose would be on a funeral.

It's art class. Mrs. Hennessy shows us a painting by the

surrealist artist René Magritte that depicts an old-fashioned smoking pipe. Below it are the words *Ceci n'est pas une pipe.* This is not a pipe.

I remember my classmates laughing. We thought this was some kind of weird joke. But the teacher explained what Magritte was trying to say: A picture of something is not the thing itself. Then we talked for a while about sensual perception and Plato's allegory of the cave, which says that all that we can see of the world is nothing but shadows of reality. It had happened more than once that Mrs. Hennessy turned art class into philosophy class. According to her, great artists have always been great philosophers at heart.

I'd never have thought that her art class, of all things, would offer practical help in one of the most critical moments of my life.

This is not Minecraft.

The Enderdragon comes at me with glowing eyes.

This is not a dragon.

I stare back at him.

Just before he reaches me, I let myself fall back. His head shoots over me only inches away.

I embrace the monster's long neck, clawing my fingers into his scales. Only now I realize that the dragon is not rectangular, and that I have hands and fingers to grab him.

I'm carried away. The Enderdragon rises high into the air, confused and angry. I manage to move one leg up around his neck and pull myself up until I ride on his neck, grabbing his horns as handles.

The dragon is not amused. He tries to shake me off. Diving straight down, he makes a somersault and passes very close to an obsidian pillar, trying to scrape me off.

But I hold fast.

I can feel his powerful muscles, his slow heartbeat that seems to be in sync with my own. I'm one with him as we speed through the air.

I'm riding the Enderdragon! Too bad I won't be able to brag about it.

A strangely exuberant feeling befalls me. I heard that in death, the brain releases large amounts of endorphins, "happiness hormones" that sweeten the departure from life. Maybe that is what makes me laugh out loud.

Then I think of Amely, and the feeling of happiness vanishes like a defeated enderman.

This may be the End, but I'm not dead yet. Maybe I can somehow signal to the doctors that my death is not natural. Maybe I can leave some kind of sign. If they realize that something's wrong, they might examine me thoroughly. Then they'll find the poison that killed me. They will call the police, which in turn will investigate my case. The nurse will testify that she found Amely's stepfather at my bed, outside of visiting hours. They will interrogate him and the truth will be discovered.

Then Amely will be freed from her imprisonment. My death will be meaningful.

But how am I going to achieve that? Surely not by flying around here.

I bend forward, whispering into the dragon's ear, "Listen, dragon, you must help me! I need to find an exit from the End!"

I hear a voice cold as ice directly inside my head. "Then you need to kill me."

"But I don't want to kill you! I'm sick and tired of fighting! Can't we work together as a team, you and me?"

"You are a mortal. I am death. How could we ever work together?"

"Simple. You help me wake up just for a brief moment. Afterwards, you can do whatever you want with me."

"You'll die."

"I know. But before that, I have to do something."

"What do you want to do?"

"I don't know yet. But I must wake up, even if it's only for a brief moment."

"Why should I help you?"

"Because that's the only way to get rid of me!" In order to make my suggestion more attractive to him, I wedge my fingers between two of his scales, pulling on them.

"Stop that! You're tickling me!"

"I'll stop as soon as you show me an exit into reality!"

"There is no exit," the Enderdragon answers. "And there is no reality."

"Stop philosophizing. You know what I mean!"

The Enderdragon sighs. "All right. Hold fast!" He beats his wings heavily, rushing toward the edge of the End island. Beyond, there's only blackness.

"What are you doing?" I ask. "Where are you taking me?"

"I'll show you what your situation really is. Maybe then you'll leave me alone."

We fly out over the edge of the island. As I turn, I see the endermen gathering at the edge, staring at us.

The island diminishes until I can't see it anymore. But the dragon still beats his wings heavily, accelerating. Although I can't see anything, I have the sensation of moving incredibly fast.

I stare ahead, but there's nothing to see. Instead, I feel

my life energy dwindle. I try to take another potion of healing, but the items in my head have vanished.

I look down at myself. Instead of diamond armor, I wear a thin hospital gown. I don't carry anything else with me.

"Please hurry," I say. "I haven't got much time left!"

The Enderdragon doesn't answer.

I don't know for how long we glide silently through the darkness. I'm getting tired. I want to close my eyes and lie down on the smooth scales of the dragon, just for a short time.

No, I shout at myself. You mustn't fall asleep!

But my eyes grow heavier and heavier.

Then I see a small spot of light in the distance. I focus on it, wish myself toward it, and it does grow slowly.

The spot takes the form of a hospital room. For a moment, I'm happy about it. Then I realize that something isn't quite right.

The perspective is wrong. Instead of seeing the room from within my bed, I'm looking down at it from an angle, as if looking at a bed of a dollhouse.

The room grows quickly. I'm falling toward the bed, which is now giant size. I grab the dragon's horns, expecting to crash into the bedspread. At the last moment, the Enderdragon flaps his wings and swoops up. Now we're gliding along the surface of the bed at a dizzying speed, as if flying over a snow-covered landscape.

A chain of hills rises up before us. As the dragon climbs its flank and flies over it, I recognize it as a fold in the covers.

Higher and higher the dragon climbs, until I feel as if I am looking down on a sleeping giant from miles high. His eyes closed, the giant looks so peaceful. As if he's having a deep, sweet dream.

The giant is me.

"We need to wake him up!" I shout.

"That won't work," the dragon replies.

"Fly to his ear!"

The dragon obeys. The outer ear is enormous, the auditory canal large enough to fly into.

"Wake up, Marco!" I shout as loud as I can. But in this giant ear, my voice is no more than the faint buzz of a mosquito in the distance.

I wonder whether it's a good idea to fly into the ear. Maybe this way I can get into my own brain, regaining control of my body. On the other hand, this doesn't sound extremely plausible to me, and my ear doesn't look very clean anyway.

I direct the dragon to one of the eyes. The eyelashes rise up like thin tree trunks. I try to grab one and pull the eyelid open, but even the might of the Enderdragon isn't enough for that.

Suddenly, a kind of earthquake shakes the ground beneath me. The eyelid has twitched. Apparently, I have triggered a reflex.

I pull at the eyelash a second time. Again, there is a brief earthquake reflex, but the eye remains shut.

This won't work. Even under normal conditions, my sleep is very sound. Now my body is overdosed with a sleep-inducing drug.

I look around in desperation. In the distance, medical instruments rise into the sky like a mountain range of metal and plastic. There's a large screen with a glowing line that's disturbed by spikes that glide slowly to the left. Each time a spike appears on the right end of the screen, a beep sounds. The intervals seem quite irregular to me.

A wire is running down from the screen, along the arm of the sleeping giant, until it vanishes below the white plain of the bed cover.

I get an idea. "Come on!" I shout at the Enderdragon. "Fly me down to that arm!"

"Don't you get it?" he asks. His icy voice sounds a bit annoyed. "You can't do anything! You're just a thought!"

"We'll see!" I answer stubbornly.

The Enderdragon does me the favor. We're landing on the giant arm, close to the crook.

I climb down from the dragon's neck and walk on the skin, which looks like an irregular plain from this perspective. Holes are scattered across the ground with thick hairs rising from them, each longer than me.

I grab one of the hairs and pull.

A tremor runs through the ground I'm standing on. I lose my grip and almost fall into one of the pores.

I gather myself up and pull at the hair again. "I'm a spider!" I shout at the top of my voice. "A nasty little hairy spider, crawling along your arm! Come on, spiders scare you witless!"

Again, there's a tremor, even stronger this time. I can barely hold on to the hair.

The Enderdragon watches me with an expression that I interpret as pity.

"Come on, help me!" I shout. I jump up and down a few times. "I'm an ugly hairy spider!" I cry. "I'm crawling along your arm! Wake up, you idiot!"

Again, there's a shudder, but the giant remains asleep.

It's useless. I can trigger some reflexes, but I can't wake him up.

Tired, I sink to the ground. I'm finished. I gave everything I had. It wasn't enough.

I turn around. I want to thank the Enderdragon for carrying me to this place. But he isn't there.

As I look around, I see him circling high above me. He glides down and lands a short distance away on the arm, exactly in the crook. He digs his four legs in the fleshy ground, pounding down rhythmically with his head, tail, and both wing tips.

Eight touch points, like the eight legs of a spider.

I'm thrown through the air. I crash down, grab a hair, and hold on to it for dear life. I lose my orientation, unable to tell up from down. The arm lifts straight up. I can see the sheet far below me. Then there's a heavy jolt, as my sleeping self swings his arm around, trying to shake off the imaginary spider.

The giant cable connecting the arm to the heart-rate monitor is pulled out of its plug. A loud, continuous beep sounds.

I tumble down. Deep below me, in the bed cover, a dark hole appears, growing while I fall toward it. It will devour me, but I don't care.

I'm so tired ...

The last thing I hear before I lose consciousness are hasty footsteps in the corridor.

22.

Something's wrong, but I don't know what.

I don't even know how I know that there's something wrong. It's just a strange feeling that the world isn't quite like it should be.

The world is a bed in the middle of a brightly lit room. There are people standing beside the bed. I can only see them as blurred shapes. There's a beeping sound coming from somewhere to my left.

Now I recognize what's disturbing me: The world is soft and round. Instead of neat, straight cubes, irregular shapes surround me.

"Marco!" one of the people beside me shouts. I think I recognize the name. I also recognize the girl shouting it. It's Amely.

I turn my head in her direction. Now I can see her face a little better.

She's crying.

"Marco!" she shouts again. "Oh, Marco!" She bends over me, embraces me, presses her face into my chest. Her hair smells good.

I want to stroke her back, but I can't move my arm. Or can I? With an enormous amount of willpower, I manage to raise it a little, before it sinks down again. Why is it so heavy?

Amely pulls herself up, looking into my eyes. Tears fall down from her cheeks onto mine. It tickles me.

"Can you hear me, Marco?"

I try to speak, but my throat is dry. I can only produce a hoarse croak. It's important that I tell her something, but I can't remember what.

"He's needing more rest," another person says. "You better let him sleep a little more." That person wears a white coat, which frightens me for some reason. And suddenly I remember what I must tell Amely.

"T-the ...," I stammer.

She bends forward. "What?"

"The ... enderman ... where ..."

"Enderman? I don't know what you mean!"

Darkness creeps up at the edge of my vision, eats up reality like gooey black slime. I fall backwards into a tunnel. I try to hold on to this world, but I can't find a grip.

23

When I awake the next time, the world finally is as it should be. Apart from a tremendous headache.

My parents are standing beside my bed. My father, who left us years before, looks older than I remember him.

When my mother sees me opening my eyes, she embraces me for a long time. She cries on my chest as Amely did.

I touch her shoulder. My arm feels lighter now. "Amely ...," I say.

My mother draws back from me. "She's well," she says. "She's sleeping right now. She was sitting at your bed without pause for two days."

I shake my head. That's not what I meant. "Amely ... stepfather ..."

My mother's expression changes. Right away there's a fury in her eyes like I never saw before. It reminds me of the cold glow of the enderman's eyes. "Don't worry, they arrested that bastard," she says. Again, tears burst from her eyes. "He almost killed you! And I ... I trusted him ..."

"The police want to ask you some questions," my father says. "They asked us to tell them when you're ready to speak to them."

My mother sends him a black look. "Can't you see that the boy needs rest!"

"No," I say. My throat still feels dry, but the coordination of my vocal cords, tongue, and lips is working more or less. "I want to talk to them now!"

"Are you sure?" my father asks. "If you want, I can ask Dr. Stone ..."

My mother glares at him. "Don't let that scumbag come

near me!"

I remember Dr. Stone being the lawyer who worked for my father during the divorce.

He visibly shrinks. "I'm sorry, I just ... I just wanted ..."

Everything is as usual – quarrels and fights wherever you look. In this respect, there's not much difference between the Cubeworld and reality.

"I don't need a lawyer," I say in an attempt to end the controversy. "I'm just going to be answering questions!"

An hour later, a genuine police detective sits beside my bed, together with a psychologist. They ask me a lot of questions. I tell them that I was paralyzed but able to see and hear everything around me. That Amely's stepfather was here two times, alone. That he injected something into my left arm the second time. I even point out the spot where the needle entered.

I leave out the description of my adventures in the Cubeworld. The police probably won't try to prosecute all kinds of undead, creepers, endermen, and a Wither, even though they are certainly guilty of criminal assault, unlawful detention, and attempted murder.

It gets interesting when they ask me how I managed to pull the cable out of the cardiac monitor, even though I was completely paralyzed. In favor of simplicity, I say that I can't remember. They accept it without further questions.

The police detective is so kind as to answer some of my questions as well. After the doctors discovered that someone had tried to poison me, they called the police, who soon found out about Amely's stepfather being in my room outside of visiting hours. When Amely heard about the attempt on my life, she told them everything. Amely's mother was admitted to a clinic after a nervous breakdown.

Supposedly she had no idea what her husband did to her daughter. Amely's stepfather was formally accused of child sexual abuse and attempted murder, which, when convicted, will keep him in jail for the rest of his miserable life.

When the police detective and the psychologist finally leave, my mother comes back into the room, together with Amely.

The rest of the story is a little sugary, and I never liked that kind of happy ending. Therefore, I'll leave out the part where we embrace each other, where Amely tells me that I saved her life, where we kiss, and all that.

Instead, in closing this tale, I'll offer a final piece of advice: Watch out for the enderman!

Did you like this book? If so, please tell your friends and fellow Minecraft players about it! You can also like it on facebook.com/Cubeworldnovel, mention it in your blog or on twitter, and e-mail me any questions or comments to karlolsberg@googlemail.com.

Thank you for your support!

Karl Olsberg